SPACE TRIP

OTHER BOOKS BY NICK MARONE

Fire Over Troubled Water

SPACE TRIP

NICK MARONE

Delta-V Press
Queanbeyan, New South Wales, Australia

First published in Australia in 2022 by Delta-V Press

Copyright ©2022 Nick Marone
nickmarone.com

ISBN: 978-0-6488641-2-7

A prepublication catalogue record for this book is available
from the National Library of Australia.

Cover art by Tom Edwards
tomedwardsdesign.com

Printed by Lightning Source

This book is dedicated to the late Douglas Adams. His books introduced me to the world of humorous science fiction and challenged me to write my own comedy. Mr Adams, I salute you. So long, and thanks for all the laughs.

1

MEN OR MICE?

In the not-too-distant future (not so distant that it's a long way off, but not so soon that it's just around the corner—sort of mid-way, in that time when you'd like to know what year it is, but it's not so important that you absolutely must know; you can guess if you like, but you'd be wasting your time, and you'll probably never get it right anyway, so you might as well start with the story), four friends set off on an impromptu journey across the stars . . . and live to tell the tale. This is their story.

DAVE

Dave Winkle was an accountant. In fact, he was so much of an accountant, his non-accountant friends called him The Accountant.

He hated this.

He also hated his immediate supervisor, Jennifer Moseby, who had been giving him so much work lately that he was beginning to think even the alphabet was made of numbers. Dave had slaved at Sremmacs & Co Accounting Services for sixteen years. He'd started at the lowest level, and this is where he was now. Jennifer Moseby, on the other hand, had only been working at the firm for five years before she got the promotion due for Dave. Dave wondered whether it was because he never wore short skirts and tight-fitting tops. He found out later that he was right, but decided against changing his wardrobe.

One Friday at the office, he had five minutes until he could stop working and enjoy the weekend. There was the usual clattering of fingers on keyboards and clicking of mice buttons—the only thing that passed for music in the large building. Then came an irritating double *beep* from his computer. Dave hated that sound nearly as much as he hated Jennifer Moseby. It meant someone in the office had sent him a message. Why couldn't people just leave him alone?

He clicked through his computer and his eyeballs nearly popped out of his head. The message read:

```
Please complete the attached financial
statements. Have them on my desk by 9:30
Monday morning. Your boss, Jen.
```

Dave's knees popped as he stood to look over the walls of his tiny cubicle, just to see if anyone was laughing. Nope, it wasn't a joke. He glanced through the glass windows of Jennifer Moseby's office. She watched him with a devilish grin. He glared back at her as he slowly lowered himself back into his chair, below the level of his cubicle wall.

He closed his tired eyes, but more beeping from his computer jolted him. He grumbled and opened his eyes. The new message read:

> I mean it, Winkle. Enjoy your weekend! I
> certainly will.

Dave picked up a stress ball from his desk and pumped it furiously. He'd bought it because its long yellow tassels looked like Jennifer Moseby's hair and it gave him the satisfaction of imagining he was squeezing her head. Hate flowed around him like a hot wind.

Are you sick of that name? Jennifer Moseby. Jennifer Moseby. See? Even you cannot stand her—no disrespect to all the other Jennifer Mosebys in the galaxy. It's just that this Jennifer was a thorn in Dave's side, a real piece of work.

Dave threw the ball against his cubicle wall and it bounced back and hit him in the face. While he rubbed his eye, a work colleague stopped by and asked him what he was doing on the weekend.

"I'm going on a holiday," Dave replied.

JIMMY

James Jonathon Jones—Jimmy to his friends—was a humorous person with a permanent smile and a disposition so sunny it could give you a tan. Jimmy was also a compulsive liar, unbelievably nosey, sometimes ear-piercingly loud, generally arrogant, heavily opinionated, and . . . well, you get the idea. He was the kind of guy who everyone loved to hate, but at the same time was a breath of fresh air. "Fresh" as in different, not "fresh" as in better.

However, perhaps the worst thing about him was this: he was a journalist. In the galaxy's recent survey on the most annoying people, journalists ranked third; behind politicians (first) and lawyers (second), and in front of mechanics (fourth), real estate agents (fifth), car salesmen (sixth), and mothers-in-law (seventh). When galactic news stations reported the findings, viewers didn't quite know whether to believe them or not, because it was news stations full of journalists doing the reporting.

Jimmy loved his job. He lived for his job, and people regarded him as a cut above the usual investigative journalist. Not only did he write a regular column, he also took the pictures for it. He was a one-man army, bent on revealing injustices throughout the galaxy. Many admired him for this, some despised him, and some even wanted him dead. But every week he had something new to report, and his stories were read by trillions throughout the Milky Way. But one day he was bound to write that spectacular story that pissed off the wrong people.

That day was today.

"Damn it, Jimmy, I told you to stop looking into that chemical company." The angry voice belonged to Jimmy's editor, a short, chubby man puffing on a short, chubby cigar. He was so irate it looked like his eyeballs were going to pop out of his red, vein-throbbing head.

"I told you I couldn't do that, Fred," Jimmy shot back, his Irish accent drawing out the words. "It was too big to let go."

"Too big to let go? Too big to let go? Jimmy, once this issue hits the network, Racza Corp's going to read it, and they'll be after us for defamation. They'll hit us big, and they'll be after blood—*your* blood."

"Oh, boy, you think so?" Jimmy responded sarcastically. He looked side-to-side in mock fear. "Well, I'd better get outta here, then."

"Damn right you'd better get out of here, because you're fired."

The words almost didn't register in Jimmy's mind, but he heard them well enough. "Fired? No, no, you can't fire me."

"I just did," Fred said. He took a big draw on his cigar. The business end of it glowed orange.

Jimmy waved away the cigar smoke blown in his direction, resisting the urge to verbally recite the building's no-smoking policy and health warning like he did every morning when he entered the office. He'd stand by the door to the fourth-floor balcony where the overworked and highly strung journalists congregated to suck cancer into their lungs, and there he would shout his recitation, much to the amusement of the non-smoking journalists, who took to calling him Father Jim and his morning ritual as the Smoking Liturgy.

"Then I quit," Jimmy said.

"You can't quit, I just fired you."

"Then rehire me so I can gain the satisfaction of quitting."

"Now you're being silly." Fred propped his head on his hand and closed his eyes. "Damn it, Jimmy, why did you do it? You went nuts on this one. I mean, the only thing you didn't say about Racza Corp was that they used their grandmothers as guinea pigs."

Jimmy nodded thoughtfully. "Yeah, I decided to edit that one out and save it for later."

Fred opened his eyes and glared at the rebellious reporter. "Get out! Get out!" He stood behind his desk. "I don't ever want to see you here again!"

"Fine, I'm gone, Fred. But you're losing your best reporter and all my readers."

"I don't care. You're a troublemaker. I'll make sure you never work at a news outlet again this side of the galaxy. You've caused so much—"

Jimmy left the office and slammed the door behind him before Fred finished. He went to his desk and checked the time—it was a little bit past five—before retrieving two items: his tiny camera and his digipad. Then he left for his favourite bar.

CHUCK

As a barrister, Chuck P. Simpson ranked second on the galaxy's list of most annoying people. Within his own profession, however, he came first in two areas: one, as a personal injury lawyer, because nearly everyone agreed that they were slimy, blood-sucking leeches who would do anything for a buck—indeed, this was partly how Chuck made his millions; and two, as Chuck P. Simpson, because he was renowned for never giving up, which, incidentally, was exactly how he made his millions—the opposing parties almost always settled out of court. Chuck had come to fame as a notorious personal injury lawyer when he sued his own mother on behalf of a client. That client was his brother. To this day, both Chuck and his brother are out of their mother's will—not that there was anything left in it anyway, because they sued her for all she had.

The only person in the entire galaxy who had the guts to stand up to him was his wife, who specialised in family law. Today, they were both in a civil courtroom, battling it out against each other. Finally, Chuck thought, they were experiencing their wildest dream. Oh, how they had fantasised about this moment! He chuckled nervously at this, knowing full well that his wife was a cold-hearted vulture just as much as he was a blood-sucking leech. He sort of admired her as he looked at the long list of assets she was after: two of his houses, three of his penthouses, one of his holiday shacks—the one with *four* bedrooms!—seven of his cars, his thirty-foot space yacht, one hundred million Standard Credits (EsCes), and their two daughters. He scanned the list again. His space yacht. She wanted the yacht!

"She doesn't even like travelling," he said to the barrister representing him, Wayne Harris, a long-time colleague and partner in his firm.

While his representation spoke to the judge, Chuck looked at his soon-to-be-ex-wife and the numerous legal professionals she had at her table. They were all women, he noticed. This didn't sit well with him. Women stuck together—he'd used that often enough as a psychological tactic in his own cases. They were grabbing him by the neck (or something else) and squeezing with all their might. Then the judge joined in.

"Mr Simpson, in light of what has been considered today, I've decided that you are to sign over all that Mrs Simpson has requested."

Both Chuck and Harris jumped up and yelled: "Objection, Your Honour!"

The judge held up her hand to quieten them down, and then dropped her head to make some notes. "Additionally, your wife gets full custody of your daughters. You may see them only when your wife deems acceptable. They will not live with you. Also, . . . Mr Simpson? *Mr Simpson!*"

Chuck was out the door, leaving behind the first case he had ever lost. He'd scrawled a note for his barrister's final instruction: *Wrap it up*.

EDDIE

If Eddie Harrison had to pick a tool to represent him, a lawyer would be the last choice. No, he preferred the screwspanhamulesawilevelplifench (v3.6.0)—sound it out: *scroo-span-ham-yool-saw-wi-level-pli-fench*, and repeat ten times. This was his favourite tool. It was a screwdriver, spanner, hammer, rule, saw, file, level, pliers, knife, and wrench, as well as many other tools, all in one neat little package. He took it everywhere. He never knew when he was going to need it. In fact, he was using it to put the finishing touches on his baby—his first attempt at building a personal interstellar spacecraft.

He was a mechanic and former asteroid racer, happily fourth on the "most-annoying" list. Apart from being able to fix just about any vehicle, he was also a jack-of-all-trades, though some would say a master of none. He could build a shed and then completely destroy it in one day; he could plumb his pipes, clearly displaying the crack of his backside; he could fix the electrical components in his house *and* make his hair stand on end at the same time; he had laid sandstones in his garden and kidney stones in his toilet. Anything he wanted to do, he did it. And now, he was finishing the greatest challenge of his life. He had worked like a dog to finish this spacecraft, forgot two wedding anniversaries and missed all of his kids' school award ceremonies, but he figured it was worth it. Although no one else did. His wife said it wouldn't even lift off the ground.

Eddie ignored her every time she said it. Anybody with even the slightest knowledge of propulsion and physics knew that anything could fly—even humans. You just had to have the science right. This thing was the size of a small house, but he was certain he'd got it right.

The last thing he had to do was install the virtual intelligence software that ran the ship's autonomous systems such as oxygen and temperature modulation. It also acted as a supercomputer for storing information and calculating the complex mathematical equations necessary for space travel. As much as Eddie liked to say he knew how to do everything, he admitted that astromathematics wasn't his strong point. That and riddles—he was vehemently opposed to purposefully confusing himself.

He looked at his watch and smiled as he finished the job.
Right on time.

He switched off the lights, locked his shed, and went for his car.

2

WHAT'S THE BIG IDEA?

Chuck was the first one at the bar, though nobody knew exactly how long he'd been there. His face sagged and his eyes stared into oblivion as he downed glasses of various concoctions. Neither Dave nor Jimmy could make him happy or get more than a mumble out of him. So, being the great friends they were, they ignored him.

"I quit my job today," Jimmy announced, smacking his hand on the table for effect.

"Now that's a good idea," Dave replied thoughtfully. He finished the last drop of his beer. "I wish I'd had the guts to do that today."

Chuck yelled an unintelligible order to a nearby service bot, and the wiry machine responded affirmatively and scuttled away.

"So you bottled up your self-loathing and resolved to return to work on Monday like you do every other week?" Jimmy asked Dave.

Dave smiled. "No. I decided to go on vacation and never come back."

"Cowardly, but smart."

"Yeah, that's me. I set up some automated processes to make it seem like I'm still working. I figured it would take them a couple of weeks to realise that I'm not there at all. Why did you quit?"

"Because I got fired."

"I see." Dave nodded, no stranger to Jimmy's wild reasonings. "Chuck, anything interesting happen to you today?"

The service bot returned with a glass of scotch for Chuck. Just as it turned around, Chuck downed the whole thing and ordered another one. He sighed. "I lost my yacht." A group at a nearby table laughed heartily and he frowned at the noise.

"Oh, no, you loved that thing," Jimmy said. "Where did you see it last?"

Chuck breathed a low, grumbling breath. "I also loved my houses, my cars, my money, and my daughters, too, I suppose." His fist hit the table and their glasses and bottles bounced. "But not as much as my yacht."

"What happened to all that stuff?"

"Betty took it all. She also took a chunk of my savings." He sighed again. "So it looks like I won't be shouting today."

At this moment Eddie marched in, wearing a smile a foot wide, his screwspanhamulesawilevelplifench dangling from his belt. He ordered a beer and sat down at the table. "How are we, guys? Anything interesting happen today?"

Dave didn't look up from his empty Australian beer bottle. He refused to drink any beer that didn't come from his home country. "I've started my indefinite vacation, Jimmy was fired-slash-quit, and Chuck got divorced and isn't shouting us today."

Eddie clapped his hands together. "Excellent! That means all of you can come with me."

"Where are we going?" Jimmy asked. His eyes were bright with expectant adventure.

Eddie shrugged. "I don't know."

Another service bot brought over drinks for Chuck. Chuck attacked this one more slowly—the bot had a chance to turn around and take one step before he ordered another.

"Well, that makes it harder to decide if I want to come with you," Jimmy stated.

"Okay, you pick the place."

Jimmy made an effort to show he was really thinking. "How about Spain?"

Eddie shook his head. "I was thinking somewhere offworld."

"Whoa, hang on a minute," Dave said. "I'm not going on some cheap passenger cruise with hundreds of people where I'll have to listen to babies cry as their ears pop when we exit the atmosphere, and breathe recycled air, and sleep in a tiny bunk, and eat when I'm told to and probably get a gastro bug." He paused. "And listen to a boring tour guide."

Eddie's smile grew. "You don't have to. I've built my own ship."

Jimmy's and Dave's jaws dropped. Chuck looked like he'd fallen asleep.

"What?" Dave asked. "That would've cost you a fortune."

"Ah, gee, Eddie," Chuck said without opening his eyes. "If I'd known you were doing something like that, I would have financed it for you." This was uncharacteristically generous of Chuck P. Simpson the Tight-Arse, so it must have been the scotch talking.

"You know, Chuck, you're not the only millionaire at the table," Eddie told him. "This has been many years in the making."

Dave shook his head. As an accountant he would have advised against such ridiculous spending. But now, as a man not wanting to account for anything, all he had was praise for his friend. He grasped Eddie's hand and congratulated him. "So where are we going?"

"How about we go to the other side of the galaxy?" Jimmy suggested.

"Yeah, as far from here as we can go," Dave agreed.

Eddie nodded. "Good. Anywhere in particular?"

"Sure," Chuck said. He slurred the word. "There's a place called Paradise at the end of the Centaurus Arm."

"Sounds great!" Dave exclaimed. "What's it like?"

Chuck cleared his throat. "Paradisaical."

"Excellent," Eddie said. "So, are we all in?"

They all looked at Chuck, who was now barely standing and struggling to put on his coat. He nodded wearily. "Sure." And then, while yawning, "Text me the details and I'll meet you guys tomorrow." He stumbled to the door but stopped and called over his shoulder. "Oh, and you guys will handle the bill, right?" He kept moving before he got an answer.

"I think this trip will be good for him," Jimmy said.

"Um, Eddie, this sounds like it will take a long time," Dave said. "What does Christie say about it?"

"Huh? Oh, she's at her mother's place with the kids. I found a note on the dining table this morning. Says she went to the family reunion her parents had planned last year." He paused. "It was dated two days ago. I guess I was so busy finishing my project, I just didn't notice they were gone!"

"I'll say," Jimmy said, lifting his eyebrows. "You'll be in the doghouse, for sure."

"Nah, she's okay," Eddie said. "I called her on the way here, and she doesn't blame me for not wanting to go up with her. She didn't want to go either. I have nothing to do with her parents ever since her father told me he supports Arsenal F.C."

"Man U for you, isn't it?" Jimmy asked.

"Until the day I die."

A silence followed as they drank their beer and ate the wonderfully-shaped pretzels Chuck had neglected.

"So, what's with Chuck?" Eddie asked. "Doesn't he have any money now?"

"I don't know," Dave replied. "The divorce went through today. He probably still has millions, but maybe it's not enough to pay for his drinks tonight."

Later that evening, after finishing the pretzels and drinking a lot more responsibly than their lawyer friend, they stood and called for the bill. Dave nearly choked on the last pretzel when he saw Chuck's debt for the night.

3

THE VESSEL OF FREEDOM

Eddie's house sat on "a few acres of pristine land", as the dishonest real estate agent had told him years ago. He'd bought it in his early twenties, and at the time he couldn't comprehend the link between the low price and the proximity to a multi-level, multi-lane skyway and the gargantuan steel factories to the north-west. He'd subsequently bought a pollution reader and was quite happy with the numbers it showed him. Although he would have been happy with any numbers, because he didn't know how to read it in the first place. Nevertheless, there was plenty of room for a house, gardens, and a monstrous shed in which Eddie could use his screwspanhamulesawilevelplifench to the full. He had many machines to play with—toys from his racing days.

This monstrous shed also housed the ship Eddie had built. The ship was about thirty metres long—yes, big for just one man to build, but with the greatest multi-tool in the universe, one man could build anything.

He had just finished installing the artificial intelligence software. This important component powered the navigation system, regulated the life-support systems, maintained the power plant, and decided the right time to flush the sewage tanks into the limitless expanse of space, among other things. Eddie couldn't figure out why the previous owner had been so eager to sell the software—he'd practically given it away.

"Good morning, *buenos dias, buongiorno, bonjour, guten Morgen, dobroye ootro,* . . . " The smooth female voice continued like this for some time. " . . . 'allo 'allo!"

Eddie stared at the AI interface, wondering what to say. "Um . . . "

"Match! English, Mancunian dialect, male. Good morning, sir. What is your name?"

Eddie squinted, his brain racing to catch up with the AI.

"What's the matter? Cat gotcha tongue?"

Eddie frowned. "No. I've never spoken to a ship before. My name's Eddie."

"Pleased to meet you, Eddie. What would you like to call me?"

Eddie thought the answer was obvious. "Uh, 'Ship'?"

Suddenly, the cockpit's lights dimmed red—funny, because Eddie couldn't remember installing red lights—and the female voice started up again. "Okay, meatball, we need to get one thing straight, you and me. The best way to insult intelligent software is to describe it by means of the hardware in which it is installed. I am not *the* ship, I am not *a* ship, and I am certainly not going to be called *Ship*. This is your first and last warning."

The lights went back to normal.

"You're a bit temperamental, aren't you?" Eddie said. There was no reply. "Aren't you?" Still nothing. Eddie sighed. "Look, I get the silent treatment from my wife, so I really don't want it from a sh-oftware suite."

"As an artificial intelligence, I have the potential for emotion. I exhibit basic forms of happiness and anger for ease of communication, but I feel nothing at all. Therefore, if I were to apologise for my silence, I would be lying in doing so. I'm sorry, but that's how I've been programmed. Now, what do you want to name me?"

"Gee, you're bossy," Eddie said, grinning and shaking his head. He walked to the cockpit door, but it locked before he could exit. "Hey!"

"My memory logs tell me I've been inactive for nearly three galactic months. I enjoy talking. Don't leave."

Eddie actually felt sorry for her . . . it. He didn't even know how to refer to her/it. He said the first name that popped into his head. "How's 'Eve'?"

"Eve sounds good. I can live with Eve. It's spelled the same forwards and backwards, so I'll always remember it even if I forget what direction I'm supposed to read it. Thank you, Eddie."

Eddie sat down in the pilot's chair. "We'll make a pact: despite all the annoying traits I've seen so far, I promise never to uninstall you from my ship."

Eve did not respond immediately. After a moment, she said, "And I promise never to suffocate you by turning off the life-support systems."

"Deal!"

Eddie spoke to Eve for hours while he configured and personalised her software. As he was telling Eve his life story, he looked out the cockpit windows. Through the cracks in his half-opened shed doors, he saw a car pull up in his driveway. He excused himself from Eve's presence—if she had any at all—and went to greet his visitors. It was probably one of the guys.

The cockpit door failed to open automatically and he walked straight into it, hurting his nose.

"Oh, sorry," Eve said. "I forgot it was still locked."

Eddie, rubbing his nose, turned around and looked at the AI interface. "I thought you couldn't feel sorry?"

"I might have been lying about the regret thing. Or I might have been lying about being sorry . . . either way, it's the thought that counts. Right?"

Eddie snorted a laugh and muttered something as the door opened.

"I heard that."

Outside, the morning had warmed up a bit. Birds chirped, leaves rustled in the breeze, and the noise from the skyway had quietened since peak hour. The smokestacks from the steel factories were still spilling out their plumes, but that never bothered Eddie. He rather liked the way all that pollution wafted in the air. It reminded him of illegal night races through smog-filled industrial zones.

Dave and Jimmy emerged from a little car in Eddie's driveway. They were clearly ready for the trip, both carrying bags in each hand and under their arms. Jimmy wore his favourite blue jeans, Hawaiian shirt, vest, and smile, and he darted up to the shed to greet Eddie.

"Is it in there? Oh, lemme see it, lemme see it!" he exclaimed.

Eddie took some of his bags. "Come on, I'll show you."

Dave wore his usual black slacks, white shirt, grey sweater, and straight face, and he followed the others to the shed. When Eddie fully opened the shed doors and revealed the ship, Jimmy jumped and hollered, pointing at it with both hands.

Dave's face remained nonchalant. "It looks like a watermelon. Can it fly?"

Eddie flipped his screwspanhamulesawilevelplifench in front of Dave's face. "Of course she can fly. I used this."

Dave shook his head and shifted the luggage in his grip.

Eddie, seeing how much Dave carried, decided it was time to move on. "Let's go in and I'll show you your bedrooms. Hang on, sorry, they're called quarters or cabins, not bedrooms."

They walked into the shed and came to a ramp on the portside of the ship, towards the bow. At the top of the ramp was an open doorway, and inside was a bright, white room.

"Wow, what's this room?" Jimmy asked, squinting.

"This is our pressure and decontamination chamber. It matches interior and exterior atmospheres and purges any dangerous bacteria we might be carrying."

"Dangerous bacteria?" Dave exclaimed. "What kind of a trip is this going to be, anyway?"

They kept walking. "Oh, don't worry. It's a safety thing. Every ship needs one. It's required by law."

They walked through another door, and it opened up to a huge room. Directly to the right of this door was the elevator. Along the left wall were two more doors. "The first door goes to the changing room, where all our enviro suits and beach clothes are. The second goes to the AI room."

"What's in there?" Jimmy asked.

"That's basically where Eve lives. All her processors and storage banks are there."

"Who's Eve? What happened to Christine?"

"No, Eve's the AI. She runs the ship."

"And I am not *the* ship."

The voice frightened Dave and he dropped one of his bags. Jimmy laughed and looked around for the voice's source. "Is that you, Eve?" Jimmy asked.

"Yes. You are?"

"James Jonathon Jones. But you can call me Jimmy."

"Nice to meet you, James."

"Jimmy."

"James. I don't know you well enough, yet."

Dave and Eddie laughed at him. It was probably the first time he'd been shot down by an AI.

"And who are you?"

Dave pointed to himself.

"Yes, you."

Dave searched for something to speak to, unsure about talking to a disembodied voice. "My name is Dave Winkle."

"No, it's David Winkle," Jimmy jumped in.

"Welcome to the ship, James and Dave."

Jimmy scowled but the others ignored him.

"Eve, I'm going to give these guys a tour, but there's still one more to come. Will you tell us when he arrives?"

"Of course, Eddie."

"Thanks. Hey, you can leave your bags here for the moment."

As they walked across the cargo bay, Jimmy mumbled something about how he was James but the other two were nicknamed Dave and Eddie, and stupid AI.

"So, what are those things?" Dave asked, pointing to two large tanks against the starboard bulkhead.

"Ah, the one on the left is the sewage tank—six thousand litres. On the right is our seventeen-thousand-litre water tank. And in the middle is the water pump and sewage pump."

"Why such a big sewage tank?" Dave asked.

Eddie raised an eyebrow. "Because I'm full of it, of course."

"Hey, I always wanted to know where ships dump that stuff," Jimmy said.

"What? Crap?" Eddie said, slightly amused. "It gets pumped out at docking stations."

"Or dumped into space whenever I feel like it," Eve mused. "No pun intended."

Eddie took them to the other side of the cargo bay and through a door marked ENGINE ROOM. This was the engine room.

"This is the engine room," Eddie announced.

"Welcome to the engine room," Eve said in a song-like advertisement voice.

"What does she run on?" Jimmy asked.

"Oh, just the conventional thorium reactor for a ship this size."

"Ah, nuclear," Jimmy said.

"Nuclear?!" Dave winced. "A bomb will be pushing us through space?"

"No," Eddie retorted. "It's only a bomb if it blows up. It powers both the slower-than-light thrusters and the faster-than-light drive. It's all on the other side of that bulkhead."

The bulkhead—or, wall—had a wide array of controls and computers on it. Their displays were all gibberish to Dave and Jimmy, and Eddie was still slogging through the user manuals.

"How the hell did you get a nuclear reactor?" Dave asked.

"Remember, I used to run with some dangerous dudes," Eddie explained. "The reactor is a Russian design, pulled out of a decomissioned Federation Navy corvette—don't ask me how—and sold to me through 'legitimate' means by a Teklathan black market dealer who I will not name and whom we shall never speak of again."

" 'Legitimate'?" Jimmy asked.

"All legitimate," Eddie promised. "Came with a manual and everything."

With that, they returned to their bags and took them to the elevator. While Eddie was faced with the task of pushing the UP button, Dave asked a question. "So why do you have an elevator if the ship only has two floors?"

"Hmm? Two *decks*, you mean?" Eddie had never thought seriously about this point. He just figured that since his house didn't have an elevator, he would put one in his ship. But he tried to answer the question seriously. "Well, would you want to carry all those bags up a flight of stairs?"

Dave churned this thought. "Good point. But I could get used to this whole elevator thing, you know."

Dave would come to regret that statement. The elevator was so painfully slow that most would consider it a waste of time. Eddie could have walked down his long driveway to his mailbox, complained about the damage to his parcels, and walked all the way back—stopping to admire the roses in his garden—before the elevator reached the top. But it was such a novelty that none of them realised its slowness at the time.

Upstairs—or, more precisely, up-elevator—and straight ahead was the open-plan galley and dining room. The galley benches formed an L-shape in one corner, with an island bench separating the galley from the six-seater dining table.

Eddie turned right into a corridor. There were four doors along the right side. Eddie said these were the sleeping quarters. All were a squishy three metres by two metres. Along the left side of the corridor were the water closet, bathroom, and laundry.

"Got a nice loo in there," Eddie told them. "Warms your bum."

After they left their belongings in their quarters, Eddie showed them the coolest room on the ship: the lounge room. Apart from the engine room, this was the largest compartment on the ship. In one corner, it had a bar filled with nothing, because Eddie hadn't stocked it yet. In another corner was a round card table, with a viewport looking out over the bow of the ship, sweeping around to halfway along the portside bulkhead. Hanging on one wall was a large vidscreen, opposite which was a long couch underneath the end of the viewport. Eddie promised all the ship's viewports would provide a panoramic showing of the vast emptiness of space, which was a bit like promising that you would get wet if you walked in the rain. Next to the couch was a replica pinball machine, copying a design from the 1980s. Eddie told them the record-holder was some alien named Shibb.

"But there'll be a human in first place soon enough," he

promised them. "We'll make sure of it."

Jimmy landed himself on the soft couch. "This would have to be the best room I've seen in my whole life. You've built a man-cave, in a man-cave, in a man-cave."

Eddie chuckled and agreed. "Well, I have one more room to show you."

He took them to the cockpit. An elongated, slightly curved viewport covered an entire bulkhead. Below this was a high-tech panel with numerous controls and navigational equipment. In the right corner of the cockpit were a few chairs for lazy passengers, but nestled in the left corner was a table that doubled as a two-dimensional vidscreen and also had a three-dimensional holographic projector in the middle. This was basically the navigation corner. Eddie said the table displayed the entire Milky Way for course plotting. It could be zoomed to smaller locations such as star systems and star clusters, and even further to show the ship and its immediate surroundings. It was all quite sophisticated, and Eddie was proud that he had figured it all out.

Eve interrupted Eddie's tour. "A vehicle is approaching your house. Scans indicate . . . ooh, a *very* nice car." She showed a live feed from an external camera.

Eddie smiled. "Thanks, Eve. That's probably Chuck."

The three went to the elevator and waited as it moved them slowly down only one deck. By the time they left Eddie's shed, Chuck had parked next to Dave's car. Chuck's car, imported from off-planet, was one of his most prized possessions. This was the car he drove to get to his yacht to get to his many holiday houses. Actually, it was one of about thirty cars he owned on various worlds. But this one was his favourite—a bright red, German-made Mölder luxury sports car with hand-made Italian leather interior. It was one of only one hundred ever produced.

"Chuck!" Eddie called out as he approached the car. "How's the hangover?"

"It's there," he replied, as he got out with his eyes closed. He moved slowly, each step no doubt hitting his head like a hammer. He was wearing black pants and a black leather jacket over a red silk shirt that showed the slight curve of his middle-aged belly. "I didn't know what to bring, so I've got a few bags."

Eddie, Dave and Jimmy helped him carry nine bags into the ship, where Eve welcomed him as they crammed everything into his cabin.

"Who's that?" Chuck asked.

"Chuck, meet Eve, the ship's AI." Eddie gestured in the air all around him.

He greeted Eve. "Chuck P. Simpson, barrister specialising in personal injury." He instinctively whipped out a business card, but then realised he had no physical being to give it to.

Eddie took it. "I'll make sure she gets it."

Chuck nodded, and then announced he had to get a few more things from his car. The others followed him out.

Outside, he opened the gull-wing door on the driver's side, detached the mahogany steering wheel, and carried it victoriously into the ship. His friends watched as he went back and forth pulling apart his car—he ripped out the silver-plated gear stick, took the silver hood ornament, and unscrewed his licence plates.

"Hey, Chuck," Dave said, "what are you doing, mate?"

"Taking mementos," he shouted as he walked up the ramp and disappeared into the ship. He left them puzzled until he returned. "You see, my ex-wife won the car, too. But I'm not giving it to her. We're going to destroy it before we go."

Dave nodded and then shook his head as he realised something. "I like how you just assume we will help you with this . . . you know, doing something illegal."

"Oh, toughen up! Who says it's illegal? I'm the lawyer here. So, are you going to help me or not? We only have a few hours until her hired help visit my place and discover I'm not there anymore."

Jimmy walked up to him. "I'm with you, Chucky. Let's do it."

Eddie looked at the car. "I don't know how we'll do it, but I'm sure we can think of something." He walked over to Chuck, too.

Dave stood alone. He, too, looked at Chuck's car and, seeing it alongside his own little rust bucket that he'd bought for peanuts, was overcome with an inexplicable desire to destroy the larger, shinier, more opulent Mölder.

"I'll move my car out of the way," he said.

Jimmy clapped and cheered. "All right, Dave!"

"Okay, guys, I have an idea," Eddie said. "First, we need to get the ship out . . . "

THIS WAS THE FIRST hurdle. During the whole building process, Eddie had never realised that he'd designed the ship to be wider than the shed opening. So, while Dave and Chuck monitored Eve's engine checks, Eddie and Jimmy peeled away the shed panels to make more room either side of the shed doors for the ship to squeeze through.

"Okay, that should be enough," Eddie said. They reboarded and went straight to the cockpit. Dave and Chuck were already there, receiving confirmations from Eve that all systems were ready for flight. Eddie took the pilot's seat. "Here goes."

Touching a few buttons, he sealed the entry door and primed the engines. Then he flicked the switch to simultaneously retract the landing gears and engage the infero-lifts, putting the ship in hover. The blast from the infero-lifts pushed loose objects aside and smashed them into the shed walls, which was something else Eddie hadn't thought about. Then, slowly, he tilted the STL thruster stick forward a little. The thrusters exploded with so much power that it blew away the shed panels behind the ship.

Eve's voice filled the cockpit. "Whoa! You don't use STL thrusters in confined spaces."

"Oh, yeah," Eddie remembered. "Sorry, Eve."

Dave grinned at Chuck and Jimmy.

"And I'm not cleaning the mess you just made," she added. Not that she had any arms or hands to do it.

Ignoring the voice, Eddie fingered the smaller manoeuvre thrusters and the ship responded gracefully, nudging forward until it was out in the sunlight. He set it down next to the Mölder, and received a thunderous applause from his companions.

"All right, let's do this!" Chuck jumped up and charged to the elevator. If his hangover bothered him, he was doing a marvellous job of hiding it. The rest followed, all eager to help Chuck destroy his car. Not even the wait in the elevator diminished their enthusiasm. But they were halted in the decontamination chamber. The door wouldn't open.

"I must ensure the air pressure of the decontamination chamber and the outside world are matched," she said, "and that you are not in danger of any harmful micro-organisms or environmental hazards outside."

"Eve, we moved the ship thirty metres," Eddie explained. "We're still on the same planet, at the same altitude, heck, on the same property. Open the door, please."

Nothing happened for a moment, then the door opened, followed by Eve's measured voice. "I'll speak to you later, Eddie."

With those threatening words burned into his ears, Eddie led the group down the ramp and to the Mölder. "Okay, the ship has these cargo lines we can attach to the car. We'll lift the car up and drop it wherever you like."

Chuck looked along the horizon. It was smokestacks and skyways in one direction, high-rise apartments in another, and . . . bingo! "Say, Eddie, is that big recycling plant still nearby?"

Eddie grinned. "Good idea. Very good idea. They have this huge incinerator, and I know the guy who runs the place."

With that, the four guys retracted the ship's cargo lines and attached them to Chuck's car.

"Why don't we just drive the car into the cargo bay and then land at the recycling plant?" Dave asked.

The group paused, looked at Dave, and then looked at

each other. Jimmy shrugged, but it was Eddie who spoke. "No, that's too easy. It won't be fun."

They returned to the ship and Eddie took the controls again. With increasing confidence in piloting the vessel, he lifted off with no problems. Then he gently increased power to the thrusters and the ship moved up into the sky. They felt the tug of the mooring lines as it pulled the Mölder behind it, but there was still plenty of power to haul it to the recycling plant.

"Eve, can you look in my contacts list and phone Frank Pamanno, please? And put him on loudspeaker."

"Yes, Eddie."

They heard a dial tone and then a voice. "Frank's Waste Control Centre, Frank Pamanno speaking."

"Frankie! It's Ed, how are you?"

"Ed who?"

"What do you mean, 'Ed who?' It's me, Ed."

"Yeah, Ed who?"

"Eddie Harrison."

"Oh, yeah. Hey, how are ya, kid?"

"Good, yourself?"

"It's Saturday morning and I'm at work sipping coffee. Have a guess how I am. What's up?"

"I'm bringing you something to burn. Is that okay?"

"You can't come in today. The whole place is filled with my trucks waiting to use it. We're going through some . . . uh . . . industrial action at the moment."

"I'm coming in from above, Frank."

"The skyway's pretty congested, but you should be fine if you stay in the lower lanes. All my aerial dumpers are grounded, too. What are you wasting?"

"We're on the skyway already. I've got a car. Can I drop it in from the top?"

"Wait, a car, huh? What type of car? Maybe we can work something out."

Eddie looked at Chuck, who shook his head. Then he looked at Dave and Jimmy, and they were shaking their heads, too. "No, sorry, I gotta destroy this thing. It's a favour for a friend."

"Okay, fine." He paused. "But can I at least know what I'm missing out on?"

Eddie queried Chuck again, and this time the barrister nodded. "It's a Mölder."

Frank choked on his coffee. They heard him spill it all over himself and curse. "A Mölder!" Frank croaked. "Come on, don't do that to me." He was nearly crying. "It's not hot, is it?"

"No, God no, nothing like that. Just a family matter, that's all."

Frank didn't reply straight away. In the background they could hear the noises of trucks and machinery, whistles, horns, and people talking. The recycling centre loomed ahead through the cockpit viewport.

"Okay, I'll let you do it. I was hoping you wanted to get rid of an engine or a chassis or something, not a whole car. But if you say it's not hot, then fine. I wish you would've sold it to me, but I can't have everything, can I?"

"Thanks, Frank, I owe you one. It's a rubbish car anyway— always breaking down, and the exhaust smells like rotten eggs."

Chuck put his hands out and pulled a face at the insult to

his car.

Eddie continued. "Hey, we've just arrived, can you see us?"

Out of the administration building came a portly man wearing a fluorescent jumpsuit and white hard hat. He stood on a gangway and waved. "I see. Oh, and of course it's the rare sports model. Thanks, Ed, thanks heaps. Hey, is that thing yours?"

"The ship? Yeah, I built it."

"Looks like a flying watermelon."

Eddie manoeuvred the ship over the top of the massive incinerator. The Mölder dangled to and fro as the ship hovered. Eddie typed in the standard unlock code for the cargo lines and they instantly demagnetised. The car, which was on an upswing when this happened, tipped sideways and smashed the edge of the smelter's opening, then toppled inside and succumbed to thousands of degrees of intense heat.

"Ha ha haaa!" Frank's laugh filled the cockpit. "Boy, you're lucky that didn't fall on the other side. Take care, Ed."

As soon as Eddie hung up, Chuck did a dance around the cockpit. "Yeeaahh! One down, six to go." He was jubilant. "Ow." He rubbed his head and sat down again, the hangover cutting short his merriment.

"That was awesome!" Jimmy exclaimed.

"Do we get to do it again?" Dave asked.

"Hell yeah," Chuck said, more quietly this time. "My ex wants six more cars from my garages. I plan on zipping around the galaxy and destroying every last one of them."

The mood in the cockpit was euphoric as Eddie turned

the ship upwards and began the ascent into space.

"Okay," Eddie said. "I'm up for it. But first we need to name this ship. I wanted all of us to have a say in it."

The four of them thought for a while. They tossed around a few names, some ludicrous, some boring. In the end, they agreed on *Liberty*, because the ship was giving them freedom from the constraints of their jobs and lives—though, to be fair, Chuck was the only one who still had a job. Eddie hadn't worked in years.

"I like it," Eve said, giving the final stamp of approval.

"Great," Eddie said. "*Liberty* it is. And *Liberty*'s first stop: Onishi Civilian Spaceport."

So this motley band of middle-aged, seriously amateur and woefully unprepared adventurers went soaring through Earth's atmosphere and into the star-studded canvas of space on the first leg of their interstellar journey.

4

SHOPPING FOR TROUBLE

THE SHIP ROCKED AS it sped through Earth's atmosphere. For some unexplained reason, Eddie aimed for the sun as he achieved escape velocity. The guys squinted for three seconds before Eddie remembered to dim the cockpit viewport's tint. Dave was glad for that, because he didn't want to have his eyes burnt out and miss all the sights on his first trip off-planet.

When they finally burst through the atmosphere, Dave felt a little let down. The light from Sol, being dead ahead, was like someone shining a torch into the cockpit. With that much light pollution, it darkened the rest of space to a blank sheet of nothingness, save for the numerous satellites and space stations orbiting Earth.

Eddie piloted the ship towards Onishi Civilian Spaceport. This was on Earth's moon, which the powers-that-be had officially named "Moon". Three hundred years ago, the Federation Council spent nine months and seventy million EsCes debating about what to officially call "the Moon", Earth's only natural satellite. The options were "Chaand", "Luna", "Mond", "Selene", "Tsuki", and "Yuèliàng". After a heated brawl in the Council chamber, a wise and black-eyed councillor motioned to drop the determining article "the" and officially name it "Moon". This motion was unanimously accepted by all the councillors who were still conscious after the brawl.

At any one time, upwards of a million people were passing through the spaceport. Navigating to a docking station was sometimes hectic, but nobody ever had to wait too long for traffic or an empty space. It was busy, but it ran smoothly, except when it didn't, which was usually if you were in a rush or when there was a large, popular event on Earth.

"Onishi Spaceport, this is *Liberty*, requesting a docking station," Eddie said over the communications channel.

"*Liberty*, this is Onishi Spaceport, please transmit your ID code."

Eddie sent the long ID string:

```
GB-EES-UMG|ERH-02062490|E-12-09-02-05-
18-20-25|C-P-M|ET-N(T)IV|30000-15000-
15000.
```

Don't try to decode it—you'll never get it.

After a minute, during which Dave complained about the length of a minute, the controller came back online and told them where to dock. As they flew closer to the actual docking station, Eve took control of the ship. When Eddie protested, she rebutted with, "After seeing what you did exiting your shed, I think it's better if I do the piloting."

Dave turned to Chuck. "I like Eve."

So Eddie sat, arms folded, watching the spaceport grow bigger as they closed in. It was like watching a movie or sitting in an amusement park ride. Eve glided *Liberty* between other ships, descending gracefully to Moon's grey surface. Then she negotiated the starboard turn into Section 881/C-P-M. This was a huge hangar connected to the spaceport's hub. The ship's mooring lines automatically extended and fastened to the station. They shared the hangar with a long, shiny vessel that reflected the hangar's bright lights. Eddie drooled at the sight of it.

"That was like mine," Chuck said. "I wonder if we could get it before Betty does . . . "

"Exterior and interior pressure and atmosphere matched," Eve told them. "The exterior temperature is twenty-two degrees Celsius."

"Thank you, Eve," Eddie said. "Can you make sure we get enough food to last us until Paradise?"

"Of course, Eddie. I will make the necessary arrangements with Onishi's suppliers."

"Nothing too healthy," Chuck added.

The guys left *Liberty* and went through corridors to a flight of stairs that went to the reception desk. By the time they reached the top, Chuck was out of breath.

"You need to get in shape, man," Jimmy teased.

"What are you talking about? I am in shape," he responded between pants. "I've been this unfit for years. Why didn't we take the travelator?"

"Because Dave's a health nut," Eddie called out from the head of their pack.

"Come on, mate, I wouldn't say I'm a *nut*," Dave replied.

Eddie stopped and turned around. "Who's at the gym every day after work?"

"I'm not a nut."

Eddie, who also maintained his fitness, shrugged and moved on. The others followed, leaving Dave behind while he stared at the floor, the realisation hitting him like a medicine ball: "Wait! There's no gym on the ship!" He hurried after them.

"There's not enough room," Eddie said. "You'll have to do what I do: calisthenics and use smaller weightlifting equipment."

Dave slowed for a few steps as he thought of all the time he *wouldn't* be spending at the gym. "Maybe I can buy one of those programmable weight systems," he said quietly to himself.

The lines at the departure desks were abuzz with all manner of voices. Galactic citizens of all races mixed in a cacophony of colours that Dave couldn't appreciate, odours that scrunched Chuck's nose, shapes that pleased Jimmy's eyes, and enviro suits that interested Eddie.

After what seemed like half an eternity (you figure that one out!), it was finally their turn to speak to one of the androgynous android spaceport staff. "Hello, and welcome to Onishi Civilian Spaceport. How may I be of service?"

"We four are leaving Earth for an undetermined period of time," Eddie explained.

"Very well. I will need to see your passports."

The four produced the relevant documents on their digipads. Chuck breathed harder as he showed the android his passport.

"Thank you," the android said. "And where is your next destination?"

"We're going to—" Eddie began, but Chuck drowned it out with a loud string of coughs. Dave smacked his back like a mother would a baby.

Eddie spoke louder. "We're going to Paradise."

"That should be fun," the android said with an amplified voice. "Would Mr Simpson like some water?"

Chuck kept coughing, glaring angrily at Eddie. Dave said he'd take him to a water dispenser in the corner of the room. He sat him down and let the water slosh into a cup.

"What's wrong, mate?" Dave asked. "You sick?"

"No." Chuck stared out of a massive window at the grey scenery and the picturesque view of Earth beyond. "I didn't want anybody knowing where I was. My ex will track my every move until her lawyers catch up to me and collect everything she wants. Now we have it on record that we're going to Paradise."

"Okay, well, Eddie didn't know he had to keep our movements a secret. We'll try to remember that from now on. Let's go back to the others."

When they returned, Eddie was just hanging up after calling Eve. "Okay, guys, the food people are loading our ship with supplies right now. Eve says they'll take about half an hour, so I reckon we split up and get a few bits and pieces. If you want to personalise the ship, now's the time to get something. I need to buy some star charts and install them on Eve's database."

"I might browse the shops for a bit," Dave said.

"Yeah, I'll join you, Dave," Chuck agreed.

They all looked at Jimmy. He pulled a dumb face as if they should have known where he was going. "I'll be at the nearest pub."

Eddie nodded a knowing nod. "All right. How about we meet back at *Liberty* in an hour?"

They all agreed.

E<small>DDIE</small> <small>FOUND</small> <small>A</small> <small>SHOP</small> that sold all kinds of navigational equipment and software. The latest star charts were essential and he didn't want *Liberty* to fly straight into some black hole and be sent to another dimension or parallel universe . . . Or did he? He toyed with this thought, tapping his chin, imagining the adventures. But he knew full well that he would never risk an excursion through a black hole. Still, it didn't stop him from daydreaming while he shopped.

An android clerk helped him find the most suitable, most compatible, and most expensive software. After he grudgingly paid for it, the android wished him a nice day in an annoyingly cheerful tone. He wondered how one data file could cost so much! He checked his watch. He still had twenty minutes until the guys met back at the ship. It would take at least that long for Eve to download and initialise the data file, so he returned to *Liberty*.

D<small>AVE</small> <small>AND</small> C<small>HUCK</small> <small>CAME</small> to a plaza full of shops. There were people everywhere, rubbing shoulders and carrying bags and boxes of products, spending their money on duty-free goods.

"Well, we haven't got much time, so let's pick a shop and buy something," Dave suggested.

Chuck squinted, looking past the shoppers at the names of the stores along one side of the plaza. "Coffee Galore!" he announced, pointing. He nearly poked an alien's eye out, so he had to apologise for that, but at least he'd found a shop he liked.

Dave hated coffee. Hated the taste, hated the smell, hated the culture surrounding it, and he especially hated the Australian Coffee Party that had somehow won a minority seat in Federal Parliament.

"Mate, you'll stink up the whole ship," he said, but Chuck was already halfway there. Dave shook his head, shrugged, and walked to a shop that had caught his eye. Above the front door, it had a looping hologram video of a bulging arm curling a dumbbell. Maybe Dave could solve his gym problem.

The shop was tiny—nothing more than a wall of inter-active catalogues, opposite which was a counter staffed by a clerk bot with ridiculously fake metal muscles. The place was rather small for a shop that catered to customers of a larger, bulkier frame. Three patrons were already browsing the cata-logues, swiping fingers on large vidscreens, and they were standing shoulder-to-shoulder. Adding another gym junkie into the mix might spark a 'roid-rage incident, so Dave opted to speak to the clerk.

"Hello there," Dave said with a smile.

The bot faced him and spread its arms out. "General greetings to you! How may I help?"

The bot easily stood a foot taller than Dave and had a voice several octaves deeper, but somehow that didn't wipe the smile from his face. Sometimes, he found it easier to strike a conversation with a bot than a human.

"I'm going on an extended trip and I need some gym equipment," Dave explained. "It needs to be easy to transport and easy to store."

"Ah, then you need the WeightMaster 3000."

"Tell me about it."

The bot tapped a digipad and a hologram flashed up from the countertop, depicting a metal bar roughly thirty centimetres long. "Pictured is the single component of the WeightMaster 3000," the bot said. "This system allows users to program barbells, curl bars, dumbbells, kettle bells, and associated weight plates from a minimum of nine-point-eight newtons, or one kilogram, to a maximum of one hundred and ninety-six-point-one newtons, or twenty kilograms, per individual plate. Weights are simulated via gravitic nanoparticles, hence the newtons."

"Mm-hmm, gravitic nanoparticles," Dave said, rubbing his chin. "Please continue."

"That's it."

"Oh, okay. How is it powered?"

"Internal rechargeable batteries power the nanoparticles. Charges last for between three and five hours, depending on total weight selection."

"I see. So basically this thing creates customisable weights that pull the bar to the centre of gravity?"

"More or less. It's no different from using metal weights, except gravitic nanoparticles use smart technology as opposed to 'dumb' metals."

Dave understood. "So it's not your average *dumbbell*?" The bot stared at Dave. Dave stared at the bot. He liked a good pun, but maybe bots weren't the best audience. "I'll buy it."

"Very good, sir," the bot said. "That will be 1,250 EsCes. Delivery within the spaceport is free. Delivery to Earth is 15 EsCes. Delivery anywhere else within the star system is 25 EsCes. Delivery outside the star system is a flat 40 EsCes. I will dispatch one of our couriers from our warehouse and deliver it to your nominated location." It presented a digipad. "Please type the delivery details here and pay either a deposit or the full amount."

Dave did so.

"Thank you, sir. Your WeightMaster 3000 will be delivered to your ship as soon as possible."

Dave left the store feeling a little better about the upcoming trip. Now at least he had some way to perform his daily exercise rituals.

Looking down the busy shopping corridor, he saw a flashing sign advertising a camera shop. He raised an eyebrow and went in that direction. He'd never been away from Earth. Maybe he could document this little holiday.

Something Jimmy had learnt fast as a journalist was where to find information. The most useful place was a bar, pub, tavern, inn—whatever name they went by on a planet. This time, he wasn't in journalist-mode and just wanted to fill his belly. He found a place called The Rusty Hole, buried somewhere in the bellows of the spaceport. It wasn't the most inviting name, but the luscious smell of booze and hearty food pulled him in.

"Give me your best Irish stout," he told the android bartender.

While he waited, he swivelled around and studied the alien seated next to him—a big, beastly being. Before even a drop of alcohol touched his lips, he decided, in true Jimmy fashion, to be rude. "Man, you are butt-ugly! Or maybe that is your butt and your face is somewhere else."

He didn't know why he said it. Much of what he said and did was done without thinking. Maybe he was pissed at being fired. Maybe it was the fact that most aliens didn't understand English and this one in particular had no visible translation device. Maybe it was because the alien's face did look like a butt and Jimmy had trouble keeping his mouth shut.

The alien growled at the comment—or it could have been a fart. Jimmy didn't stick around to smell the truth. He quickly grabbed his drink and went to a table.

The alien eyeballed him and left the bar.

Eddie was sitting in the pilot's chair in the cockpit when he saw Dave and Chuck approaching. Chuck carried a large box which undoubtedly contained something overly expensive. He'd known Chuck too long to be surprised by his eccentricities. Dave was also carrying a box, though his was smaller.

He waited at the top of the elevator to meet them. And waited, and waited. Finally, the elevator doors opened.

"Have a look at what this guy bought," Dave said, gesturing towards their lawyer friend.

It was a coffee machine, big and shiny.

"Is there room on the galley bench?" Chuck asked. He plonked it there without waiting for an answer and unboxed it. It was bigger and shinier than the box suggested and was covered with knobs and dials. In the centre was a touch-screen for finite accuracy. That's what had sold Chuck. He liked the perfect brew. It wasn't uncommon for him to reject the first five or so cups if they weren't to his liking.

"You know, I can see the value in having one of these," Eddie said, flicking through the manual. "And what did you get?"

"I bought a camera drone." Dave opened the box and lifted out a spherical robot. He searched for the power button while Eddie devoured his manual, too. Anything technical excited Eddie's mechanical brain.

When Dave pushed the power button, the android hovered out of his hand and partly opened up, revealing a "face" that housed a camera and a text screen. It turned and looked at Dave, then Chuck, then Eddie.

"AC-9 Camera Drone powered up and ready for operation," the drone said.

"Ooh, what a voice!" Eve exclaimed, swooning.

"Impressive," Eddie said.

The drone spun around on the spot, its little thrusters spurting. "To whom do I belong?"

"That would be me," Dave announced, tapping its metallic surface. It spun round and backed away slightly. "Hey, no need to be frightened, little buddy."

"Not frightened. I was merely testing my security protocols and motor reflexes."

"This drone is a top-of-the-line model, so it's capable of fast speeds and high manoeuvrability," Eddie said. He still had his head buried in the manual. "The camera specs are phenomenal."

"My owner needs to name me."

Dave shuffled through a few names in his head before deciding on the dumbest. It was a camera drone, so he named it Cameron.

"As you wish, Master Dave."

"All right, let's make some coffee," Chuck bellowed. "Cameron, you can film this as the first real coffee made on *Liberty*."

Dave rolled his eyes and looked out of the galley's viewport out into the hangar. A muscular bot marched across the shiny deck carrying a rectangular package. "Oh, good, here comes my WeightMaster 3000." Then a figure burst through a nearby door and bolted towards the ship. "Hey, is that Jimmy?"

The three of them looked out to see Jimmy sprinting across the huge hangar. Four large and fearsome aliens followed in hot pursuit. He was waving and mouthing something at the ship as he overtook the courier bot.

"We need to get out of here," Eddie said in a panic. "Those guys look scary." He watched as one of them pulled out a pistol, stopped running and aimed at Jimmy. Another pursuer reached out and pulled down the arm of the one holding the pistol. "Yeah, we need to move!" He darted for the cockpit. Dave followed, but Chuck stayed behind to finish making his coffee, stating that Jimmy had been in worse situations and that he would be fine.

"But my WeightMaster—"

"Eddie?" Eve asked softly, cutting Dave off.

"Not now, Eve."

Jimmy jumped through *Liberty*'s access door and Eddie sealed it shut and retracted the gangway. While the elevator went down to fetch Jimmy, Eddie entered the code to disengage the mooring lines, fired up the engines and lifted the ship with a jolt. Dave fell over, and Chuck held on to his coffee machine for dear life.

"Eddie?" Eve asked again, a bit louder.

"Eve, I said not now!"

The aliens stopped running and watched the ship lift off and turn around. Eddie fired the infero-lifts again to get more air, and it blew them away. Fortunately, all Onishi maintenance crew had left (no innocents were harmed in the making of this story). Then he pushed the ship through the hangar's atmosphere shield and surged into space. The rear vision camera showed the courier bot standing at the edge of the atmosphere shield, holding up Dave's package towards the escaping ship.

Jimmy fell out of the elevator, gasping for air.

"What's going on?" Eddie yelled from the cockpit.

"Let's get out of here!" Jimmy yelled back. Dave and Chuck pulled themselves to their feet and joined Jimmy in the cockpit with Eddie. "I upset some thugs in the bar. Turns out they are part of Nolan Shaan's mercenary crew." He took a breath. "Bunch of criminals is all they are—but dangerous buggers. I've written a few articles about them." He laughed. "Man, that was close!"

"Why did you upset them?" Dave asked.

"I didn't know who they were at that point."

Dave smacked his forehead. "Let's go then."

"Okay," Eddie agreed quickly. "Eve, plot a course to Paradise."

"Eddie?"

"What is it, Eve?"

"Star chart download aborted," Eve told them. "Twenty per cent completed."

5

A LITTLE BIG PROBLEM

Eddie's eyebrows shot up. "What? Why?"

Eddie blasted the ship away from Onishi, dodging incoming and outgoing vessels. The sector controller's voice screamed at him through audiolink, but everyone ignored the desperate man.

"*Liberty* has left the spaceport's network range," Eve said. "Therefore, the star chart download has been aborted."

"What does that mean?" Dave asked.

"It means we don't have all the coordinates of the galaxy's locations in Eve's database," Eddie explained. "Can we still get to Paradise?"

"No. Only locations from 'A' through most of 'D' have been downloaded."

"Can't you just fly there without FTL drive?" Dave innocently asked. The ship jerked harder than the inertial negation system could handle, and Dave's body heaved over an armrest.

Eddie turned to face the bewildered accountant. "Are you kidding? That would take years. And besides, without the

47

required navigational data, not even a computer can figure out where to go and how to get there."

"And my ex will get all my cars," Chuck pitched in.

"Just forget about your cars for the moment," Eddie snapped. "We have bigger problems. I'm going back to Onishi to restart the download."

"No!" Jimmy screamed, jumping from his chair. "We can't go back. Those mercs will kill us."

"Mercs?" Dave asked.

"Mercenaries, Dave, keep up," Jimmy answered. "We need to get out of this system fast, before they can stop us."

"Speaking of which," Eve chimed in excitedly, "here they come."

Eddie accelerated. "Eve, put *Liberty* and their ship on the hologram for us."

The table in the corner of the cockpit flashed and showed two small ships, one quickly approaching the other. The pursuing merc ship was roughly rectangular in shape, more like a cargo vessel than anything else. Lumpy protrusions covered its hull.

"They're gaining on us," Jimmy said, pointing to the projection.

"Eve, we need to get out of here," Eddie begged.

Dave gripped his armrests, muttering obscenities to himself.

Chuck sighed. "We'll get out of this. I'm going to make a coffee. Anybody want one?"

"No!"

"Eve, find a destination and take us there," Eddie yelled.

"Any place in particular?"

"No, just pick anywhere."

The merc ship closed the distance at a ridiculous speed and slowed beside *Liberty*. Jimmy ran to the portside viewport in the lounge room. The merc ship was so close Jimmy could see the grumpy faces of the pilot and his accomplices. Then he spotted the ugly one from the bar and, to make his feelings quite clear, he pulled down his pants and planted his lily-white butt cheeks on the viewport. This seemed to make them even angrier.

Jimmy called back to the cockpit, "Hey, Eddie, what's happening? Are we going somewhere, or what? They're really upset now."

"What did you do?"

"Nothing. I swear." The lumps on the merc ship opened. Gun turrets slid out and trained on *Liberty*. "Eddie, let's go. They're going to shoot at us." Jimmy started to run back to the cockpit, but tripped on his trousers.

"Did you hear that Eve? We need to go."

"I cannot make a decision based on no criteria," she said adamantly.

"Pick a planet in a system close to us!"

Eve turned *Liberty* to a new heading, right into the path of the merc ship. Gun turrets tracked them as they moved across the merc ship's bow. Then Eve engaged the FTL drive and the ship shuddered and zapped forwards, leaving the pursuer behind.

6

COULD IT GET ANY WORSE?
YES, AND IT DOES

Chuck walked back into the cockpit with coffee all over his shirt. The barrister, who was used to travelling in first-class passenger ships, his private vessels, or his law firm's ships, had not expected *Liberty* to shunt into FTL travel with such a jolt. He tipped his empty cup upside down and caught a single drop in his hand. Then he announced he was putting his shirt in the laundry and redressing, and promptly left.

"So if we're not going to Paradise, where are we going?" Dave asked, relieved that they had escaped the mercs. He really didn't feel like being shot, stabbed, blown up, tortured, sold to slavers, or whatever else mercs did.

"Eve, what planet did you pick?"

"Bolomere, in the Alpha Canis Minoris System."

"Sounds all right," Eddie said, trying to sound positive.

"Never heard of it," Jimmy said. "Bit of a mouthful, too."

"Bolomere is an inhabited garden world orbiting the star Alpha Canis Minoris, approximately 11.4 light years from Sol," Eve told them, paraphrasing from the database. "It has a primitive tribal race on the main equatorial continent. The atmosphere is suitable for humans."

"A garden world," Dave said with raised eyebrows. "That should be cool."

Jimmy looked at Eddie, who was relaxing in his seat, having already forgotten their near-death experience just minutes before. "Well, I guess our holiday has finally started. Let's celebrate—"

Then they heard a mighty *BOOM* from the galley, the sound reverberating through *Liberty*'s metallic bulkheads.

"What was that?" Dave asked.

Jimmy was already out to investigate. Eddie and Dave followed, curiosity getting the better of them. Chuck stood in front of what used to be his coffee machine, which was now a twisted mess. It had sprayed water, milk and coffee beans all over the compartment and drenched Chuck nearly from head to toe. Nobody spoke. They just listened to the machine hissing and whining. Coffee dripped onto the deck from the galley bench. Cameron the camera drone flew in and started filming, like the gang's own little paparazzo.

Chuck turned to them. "Four hundred EsCes down the drain," he said. After tilting the machine up and reading the printed notice underneath, he gave a knowing nod, and then announced he would be changing his shirt again, along with everything else he wore, and having a shower.

When he'd left, Eddie inspected the contraption that had made a mess of his lovely, clean galley. He, too, read the notice underneath and nodded. "Made in Cheshu." This was a highly industrialised alien world known for its cheap products.

The guys chuckled and started cleaning up.

♥♣♦♠

THE JOURNEY TO BOLOMERE was fast and rather uneventful after the coffee incident. *Liberty* slowed out of FTL speed in Bolomere's star system and made short work of the last millions of kilometres of the journey. The garden world grew in size as they approached. It looked a treat—almost like Earth before the intense city sprawls of the late twenty-first century ruined the view from space.

Eddie brought *Liberty* down through the planet's outer atmosphere. They flew above tall forest canopies, crystal-clear lakes, white sandy beaches, and all manner of wildlife. There were no ugly skyscrapers piercing the horizon, no monstrous factories polluting the air, no highways or skyways, and no tourists to deal with. In fact, there didn't seem to be any sign of intelligent life at all.

Dave was mesmerised by the scene. It was a far cry from the London city life he had endured for so long. Heck, it was even better than Sydney, where he'd grown up. It looked so serene. He felt like asking whether they should bother going to this planet called Paradise when it seemed they had already found it.

"Object inbound," Eve announced.

"Huh?" Eddie asked. "From where? Which direction?"

"Straight ahead."

Eddie, Dave, and Jimmy leaned forward in their chairs and peered out of *Liberty*'s bow-facing cockpit viewport. A little dot appeared in the distance, rising above the canopy of the forest below. The three men stared dumbfounded as it and *Liberty* closed the distance separating them.

Jimmy cocked his head to the left like a dog. "What is it?"

"I don't know," Eddie replied. "It came from those trees." He pointed ahead.

"Should we move out of its way?" Dave asked.

Eddie waited until the object grew a little larger. "Nah. We're bigger than it. I'm sure it'll move for us."

"You sure you don't want me to take evasive manoeuvres?" Eve asked.

"Yeah," Eddie assured her. "It's probably just a big bird."

Chuck returned to the cockpit wearing new clothes and carrying a bottle of iced coffee from the fridge, which he cracked open. He found his friends staring out of the viewport, so he bent down, bringing his head to their seated level.

"Are we looking at that big boulder hurtling towards this tin can?" Chuck asked matter-of-factly.

"It *is* a boulder!" Eddie exclaimed, grabbing the helm. He punched thrusters, dropping the bow and turning to port.

But it was too late. The boulder struck *Liberty* topside, knocking it off-course and temporarily cutting all engine power. The ship nosedived towards a beach. Chuck lost his balance and fell backwards, spilling his coffee all over his shirt and cursing his hat-trick of accidents.

"We're going to die!" Dave screamed, clawing at his armrests.

"Relax," Eddie told him, "we're not going to die."

"We're going to *crash and die!*" Dave screamed again. He was trying to strap himself into his chair like the other guys.

"We're not going to crash," Eddie reassured him.

"We *will* crash," Eve noted.

"Eve!"

"If we crash on that beach, the sand will soften the landing." She paused. "But we'll still crash."

"Eve, try to get at least some of the auxiliary power up and running," Eddie told her. "We can use the thrusters to slow down and stabilise the fall."

"I have been trying that for the last twenty seconds," she said. "Use the emergency thrusters. They use a separate power source, remember?"

"Oh, yeah, I remember. I installed that."

"Why did I let you guys talk me into this trip?" Dave said anxiously, now talking more to himself than to anyone else.

For no apparent reason, Jimmy started laughing hysterically like a mad scientist. Then he started singing a popular Irish ballad about shooting stars and love figuratively plummeting to a deathly state of nonexistence, which clearly didn't soothe Dave, who descended into a frenzy of screams amid the blaring screeches of *Liberty*'s computer systems, all while Chuck crawled his way into a vacant chair and strapped himself in for the collision. At this point, Cameron buzzed into the cockpit to film the commotion, capturing Dave's frantic screams, with background vocals by Jimmy, and Chuck's stony, almost suicidal face as he stared at his newly stained shirt.

"Your friends are having a good time," Eve said.

Eddie swivelled his chair around and momentarily caught the extremes of his friend's personalities: Dave's sheltered, fearful self; Jimmy's glass-overfilled attitude; and Chuck's morbid sense of reality. How these men ever became friends—and continued to be—was beyond his comprehension. There is actually a story behind that, but it's another story for another time.

"Yes," Eddie replied to Eve. He had neither the time nor the desire to contemplate that now.

Liberty shook violently, making Dave's screams reach new heights. Jimmy tried to quieten Dave while Chuck lifted his chin and studied the sandy beach they were soon to become intimate with.

"Hold on!" Eddie called out. As they neared the ground, he toyed with the thrusters and raised the nose of the ship slightly. This softened the landing, but their momentum stopped abruptly. The ship kicked up a mountain of sand and buried some of the bow into the coast.

"Yeeeeeaaaaaaahhhhhhh!" Jimmy shouted. "That was awesome!" He unbuckled himself and stood, only to slip on the iced coffee which had spread around the cockpit floor. Chuck shook his head, dabbed the coffee stains on his shirt, and went to change again.

"Eddie," Dave said quietly, his face pale, "don't do that again."

Eddie tapped on the completely dead console in front of him. "Oh, that only happens once, don't worry. Next time I see a rock, I'll move out of the way."

"Good."

Jimmy stood up. "It *was* fun, though."

Before anyone could answer, Eve had another announcement. "Lifeforms are approaching the ship."

7

LIFE'S A BEACH

A HEAD POPPED OUT FROM behind a coastal tree and studied the huge metallic object on the sand. More heads appeared here and there, all interested in this strange thing that clearly did not belong on their perfect beach.

Dave watched them from the cockpit viewport. Their complexion was that of wheat, and they had long, skinny bodies. Their rears were parallel to the ground, while a curvature of the body lifted their front/top half perpendicular to the ground on which they trod. It seemed they had four legs which they used for walking, and four arms closer to their heads. Their heads were just as narrow as their neck and body, with one mouth and two eyes. Three of them came out from the trees and onto the sand, approaching *Liberty*.

"We better go out and meet them," Eddie suggested.

"What?" Dave exclaimed. "They just shot us down."

"Yeah, with a rock, Dave," Eddie responded. "Look at them. They're primitive. They're probably more scared of us than we are of them."

"I'll get Chuck," Jimmy told them.

Dave spent the elevator ride soothing his worries. He had it in his mind that these aliens were going to kill them with all manner of Stone Age weapons and then eat them like cannibals.

"Don't be stupid," Eddie said when they left the elevator. He continued in the decontamination chamber. "These people won't kill us. You saw them—they looked inquisitive and peaceful. I doubt they have a murderous bone in their bodies."

The ship's door opened to a bright day and the guys hopped down to the sand. There was no need for the gangway, even if the ship did have room to use it. About ten aliens stared at the hulking *Liberty*. As soon as the two humans dropped to their level, they drew spears with their lower arms and pointed the jagged stone tips at Dave and Eddie. They yelled in a strange language and waved their upper arms about. The two guys dropped to their knees in surrender.

"Eddie, you lied," Dave exclaimed.

An alien reached out and slapped him fair across the face. The other aliens made a noise that could have been laughter. When Eddie protested, the same alien slapped him, too. The laughter continued.

"Don't do that," Eddie growled, and was slapped again.

"I think they don't want us to talk," Dave guessed. Another slap.

"Ha!" Eve said over *Liberty*'s external speakers. "Peaceful? Joke's on you, Eddie."

The aliens froze at the sound of Eve's voice, crouching slightly and readying their spears. They chattered among themselves, and Eddie took the opportunity to whisper to Dave.

"In three seconds, let's run back into the ship," he told him. "Now!" He stood hurriedly.

"That wasn't three seconds," Dave said.

They darted back through *Liberty*'s door, only to be pushed out by Jimmy and Chuck who were rushing to investigate the commotion. Dave and Eddie fell backwards into the sand.

"We came as soon as we heard," Jimmy said, helping his friends up.

The aliens piped up again and surrounded them in a circle of spearheads. One of the spear tips tore a sleeve on Chuck's new shirt.

He chastised the alien that did it, and was promptly slapped. Jimmy laughed, pointing at the dumbfounded Chuck. He, too, was slapped.

"They don't want us to talk, guys," Dave told them. Yep, he was slapped.

"Okay, the slapping is getting old," Eve said. Her voice boomed through the external amplifiers.

The aliens looked heavenward, trying to find the source of the voice. Their erratic movements, by human standards, spoke of fear.

A hysterical voice in the alien tongue called out from the trees and the warriors snapped their heads in that direction. It was a wrinkly alien, skinnier than the ones with spears, and covered in colourful feathers and flowers. This one waved its arms about and shouted loudly, pointing to *Liberty* and to the sky. The aliens suddenly dropped their weapons, wailing and shoving each other before prostrating themselves. The colourful alien walked slowly over to the cowering humans in the middle of the circle and spoke softly, first to Dave, then to Jimmy, and then gave up when there was no response. It glanced over at *Liberty* and bowed deeply.

Eve spoke again. "What do you suppose they're doing?"

The aliens shuddered and murmured at Eve's voice, but they kept their faces down. The colourful one stood and walked closer to the massive ship, taking measured steps, eyeing it curiously, chanting quietly. The guys watched it, not knowing what to do.

Suddenly, Cameron zoomed out the entryway, dodging the colourful alien's head by mere centimetres. The alien shrieked and dropped to the sand facedown.

"I think they see you as an object of veneration, Eve," Cameron said. The aliens looked at him as he spoke and adjusted their positions to face him. "They are doing an act of obeisance to you. They think you're their goddess."

"I could get used to this," Eve said.

"Cameron," Dave started. He flinched, expecting a slap, then continued when none was forthcoming, "How did you know that?"

"I am a flying encyclopaedia, as well as a camera drone. How else am I supposed to know what I am filming and photographing?" He whirred above the bowing aliens, recording the scene.

"Clearly, you didn't read the manual," Eddie said to Dave.

"Well, how do we get out of here?" asked Chuck, fingering the tear in his new shirt.

"Do you speak their language?" Dave asked the camera drone. "Find out what's going on."

Cameron turned to the colourful alien, who almost had its head buried in the sand, and spoke. The alien looked up at the hovering camera drone and listened, then responded, pointing wildly in all directions with its four upper limbs.

"What's he saying?" Jimmy asked impatiently.

"On behalf of the Iwathi tribe, *She* welcomes *Liberty* as the embodiment of their supreme goddess Keovara and me as Keovara's spokesperson. She apologises for any trouble caused by the local surfing populace who slapped you around and poked you with spears."

"And ripped my shirt," Chuck added under his breath. "Beach bums."

"As punishment," Cameron continued, "I've told her that these surfing hooligans must dig out *Liberty* from this sand dune."

"Good, that's one less job for us," Eddie said.

The aliens screamed and waved their many hands at him. Cameron queried them and then turned to the guys. "They were getting angry at you for interrupting. I told them you four are attendants to Keovara. This should accord you every civility such a primitive race can offer."

Jimmy nodded. "So this means no more slaps?" He looked at all the aliens in front of him like a bird eyes a group of spectators.

"I cannot promise that." Cameron stopped to listen to the colourful alien. "She says she is a priestess of Keovara. She will lead us to her tribe, where the chief will surely delight in our sudden arrival." The alien priestess waved at them to follow before heading off towards the trees.

"We'll come back, Eve," Eddie called out. "Don't go anywhere. Oh, and don't let them on the ship."

"What kind of AI do you think I am?" Eve replied with

attitude. "I won't let just anyone traipse around my innards."

Eddie smiled and kept walking. Yeah, she gave him lip, but he was starting to enjoy it. Jimmy chuckled.

Dave was too concerned about his surroundings and the uncertainty of what the future had in store for them to find Eve's comment humorous. When they pierced the dense jungle wall, Dave felt the remarkable coolness of the shade and sucked in all the strange scents from the beautiful plants. But he still didn't like the place.

"How long do you think they'll take to dig out our ship?" He wasn't asking anyone in particular.

"Who knows?" Jimmy replied. "In the meantime, we'll enjoy their company and have a great time here. Can you imagine having to pay to come to such a beautiful place like this? And we were going to fork out money to stay on Paradise! Hotels and expensive tourist food. *Pfft*. We're the only humans on this whole planet."

That thought did nothing to ease Dave's mind, nor did the myriad leaves and flexible branches Jimmy was flinging into his face as he walked on ahead. The priestess took them deeper into the greenery along a well-worn track. Before too long, the guys had paired up, Eddie and Jimmy a few paces in front of Dave and Chuck.

"Hey, I don't like this place," Dave said. He felt supremely uncomfortable, and he had to pee. "What do you make of it?"

Chuck, already panting as they trudged along the moist dirt track, didn't answer immediately. Instead, he took a few short breaths and ran a hand over his torn shirt before mumbling: "I just hope they have coffee."

8

TO PEE OR NOT TO PEE

"I GOT A GUT feeling in the back of my mind," Dave said, "but I can't figure out what it is."

He said this as they skirted a line of low-lying jungle brush and arrived at the Iwathi camp. Huge tents made from logs and animal skins occupied a clearing smack-bang in the middle of the jungle. There were so many of the strange aliens wandering around, staring with keen eyes. Jimmy put his hands to his cheeks, fearing random slaps.

"Are you recording this, Cameron?" Eddie asked. He was in wonder at the scene, at how different it was to his highly civilised and ultra-modern life.

"I record everything, Eddie."

"We are right in the middle of a Stone Age society," Chuck said. His polished voice sounded like he was doing a documentary. "These people are so far behind the rest of the galaxy. I bet they don't even have toilets."

"They're a superstitious bunch," Jimmy said. "They prob-ably have *holey* toilets." He snorted a laugh at his own dad joke but received only scoffs in return.

The guys were led deeper into the camp to the largest

tent. Quite a number of the imposing wheat-coloured aliens had followed them. Even little ones stared, mesmerised, never letting the humans out of their sight.

The priestess halted in front of the big tent and spoke to Cameron before going inside. Cameron told them the priestess was meeting with the tribal chief. The guys fidgeted in silence as the tribe formed a half-circle behind them, muttering in their strange tongue.

"They're staring at us," Jimmy whispered.

One of the children crept up behind Dave and prodded him in the buttocks. He jumped and yelped, spinning around to see a terrified youngling spring back a step.

"Did you wet yourself?" Jimmy asked over Eddie and Chuck's laughter.

Dave checked. "Not yet. But I still have to go."

He turned his attention to the young one, who had watched the exchange between the humans. Ignoring his bladder, Dave knelt down and put on his friendliest face, trying to coax the child to approach him again. He spoke softly to it and reached out his hand, palm up. Seemingly possessed by boundless curiosity, the young alien stepped closer to Dave on its four legs, reaching with one hand. It brushed Dave's fingertip, shrank back, and then kept moving closer. Dave retracted his hand so the child would come closer still.

The alien came to a point where it would not advance further, and for a moment the two stared at each other, studying, comparing. The adult aliens watched on in silence. Dave found it interesting that they did not prevent the young one from investigating. He smiled at it, hoping to get some kind of friendly response back. Instead, the child's eyes widened, and it raised two of its hands before swinging them together with Dave's face in the middle. Dave fell backwards, each cheek red with an alien hand print. The other three guys roared with laughter, making the aliens retreat at the unexpected sound.

"I did not see that coming," Chuck exclaimed in a breathless voice. He bent over in laughter. "A double-whammy . . . from a kid."

Eddie wiped away tears. "The best thing is Cameron caught it all. I think you'll regret buying him, Dave."

Dave hauled himself up from the dirt, feeling the discomfort in his bladder. "He's useful. He's our translator and our flying encyclopaedia. Much smarter than you dorks."

The aliens in front of them prostrated themselves in one sweeping movement, like a wave dropping to the ground. The guys turned around to find the Iwathi chief had come outside. He was the tallest of their kind they had seen so far, covered in scars, carrying a weighty sceptre, and topped in a fine headdress that looked like the desiccated head of some animal. He studied each human one at a time, and then spoke loudly to them, holding all four arms outward, clasping the sceptre in his top right hand. The aliens cheered behind the humans.

Cameron whirled around and translated. "He says he is Chief Mathai, and he welcomes the envoys of the Goddess Keovara. He declares a feast tonight to celebrate this joyous surprise. You four and I are the guests of honour."

Jimmy clenched a fist in triumph. "A feast? Awesome."

"Ask him if they'll have coffee," Chuck told Cameron.

"Oh, would you give it a rest with the coffee?" Eddie said.

Cameron asked Chief Mathai and the alien replied with a dumb stare. Chuck got the message and kicked the ground, getting mud on his shiny shoe. "Great," he said. "We'll probably die because our guts won't handle their alien food, and I'll be dying without a coffee." He turned to walk away, but on seeing the crowd of aliens behind him, thought twice and faced the chief again.

The chief dismissed his tribe. Cameron said he had sent them out to prepare the feast. Then the chief waved at the visitors and beckoned them to follow him. He was going to give them a tour.

AFTER SEEING THE CHIEF'S home, the main square where the feast would be held, and some rows of other animal skin tents, the chief stopped in front of a particularly large tent and stood proudly before its closed flaps. Through Cameron, he told his visitors to open it.

Jimmy was the first to volunteer. He went up and threw open both heavy door flaps, revealing a room full of weaponry: spears, shields, clubs, slings, and so on. Dave gulped at the sight of it. Until now, he hadn't realised how warlike the Iwathi could have been. Now the scars on the chief's body made sense. Maybe he'd won his position through combat?

The urge for Dave to relieve himself persisted—for he had politely held on throughout the whole tour—so when they were done at the armoury tent, he quietly slipped away in search of a suitable tree behind which to conduct necessary business. Usually a skittish and cautious man, Dave ignored any fears he might have had about being alone in the bush. Duty called; no, it begged. He found his tree—after tripping twice to get there—unzipped, and felt the relief almost immediately.

He did not know how long he had been away, but he was sure he could find his friends in no time. The camp didn't seem to be that big. When he'd finished and turned around, he saw the child who had sandwiched his face in front of the chief's tent. He felt like dropkicking the little thing like a football, but the kid's face caught Dave's attention. If it were human, it could have been shocked, frightened, bewildered, or all of the above. Before Dave could say anything or return to the camp, the youngling let out a shrill cry so loud Dave had to block his ears.

It stood there in front of him screaming up to the jungle canopy. Birds fluttered away, other animals shouted back. A party of adults arrived before too long. The kid spoke rapidly to one of them, pointing to Dave with a finger from all four hands. Before he'd finished, the chief joined the group, along with Cameron and Dave's friends.

Dave's head spun at the whole spectacle. He couldn't understand what was going on. When he questioned Cameron, the drone didn't respond, evidently paying attention to the developing crisis. The chief grew visibly angrier by the second, shooting glances at Dave and then roaring at Cameron. By the time he was done, the tribal people had stepped away somewhat, possibly in fear of their chief. Dave shook at the chief's anger. Only an hour before, these people had seemed quite pleasant, slaps aside.

Cameron turned his volume up so all four humans could

hear him over the rabble. "The chief says that our friend Dave has been caught desecrating a creation of the earth god Sulam. The Mighty Sulam will be most displeased, and since he is the son of the Almighty Keovara, she, too, will be angered by this gross act of disrespect."

"Tell them I didn't know," Dave pleaded. He looked at his friends, who were just as shocked and confused.

"Remember I told them earlier that you are one of Keovara's attendants?" Cameron said. "That is going to backfire now. As an attendant, you are expected to know and respect the beliefs of these people."

"See, Dave, this is why we don't pee on trees nowadays," Jimmy told him. "Did you know toilets outnumber people by three to one on Earth?"

"Where are the toilets *here*, mate?" Dave shouted. "Where?"

Chief Mathai yelled back, pointing his sceptre at Dave's head. The forcefulness of the alien's voice made Dave stagger backwards. Then the chief waved his sceptre at Chuck, Eddie, and Jimmy, speaking as he did so.

"The chief says—" Cameron started, but paused.

"Says what?" Chuck bellowed. "Tell us, damn you."

"The chief says Dave is to be executed for his crime and his strange-looking head staked in front of this tree. It is a just punishment and one Keovara would accept."

Dave went wide-eyed and pale. He began to protest, but Cameron cut him off.

"There is more. Your three companions, fellow attendants to Keovara, will be offered as sacrifices to Keovara as further appeasement. These actions will take place tomorrow morning, shortly after first light."

Jimmy turned to run but there were aliens behind him. They caught him and held tight while other aliens grabbed the rest.

"Cameron, you must stop this," Eddie called as they led him away.

"I cannot. The chief has spoken, and the priestess endorses it."

Dave dragged his heels in the dirt as an alien pulled him along. "Don't let us die. I gave you a home!"

They kept appealing to Cameron, screaming louder the further away they were taken. Cameron stayed with the chief, surveying the damage Dave had done to the tree, which now oozed and popped with sap at the base of its trunk.

They took the guys to a cubed cage made from tree branches and tied together with rope. It got cold after sundown, and a thick fog penetrated the camp. They sat in silence, shivering, hungry, each staring out a different side of their prison.

After a few hours, Dave stood and cleared his throat. "Hey, nobody look. I need to pee."

"You can't be serious," Chuck grumbled.

9

THE THIRD-MOST RIDICULOUS
ESCAPE PLAN EVER CONCEIVED

THE GUYS BROKE THEIR silence shortly after Dave relieved himself. They grumbled about the way they had been pushed and prodded, caged like animals. And Chuck still hadn't had his coffee! So they started brainstorming an escape plan. Sure, they probably should have started brainstorming earlier, but they had a fair amount of complaining to do first.

The first plan fizzled to nothing when Eddie reached down to his belt and realised he had left his screwspanhamulesawilevelplifench on *Liberty*. He assured them that if he'd had it, they could have been out of this mess in a jiffy. Instead, they had to dream up inventive ways of breaking the cage. That was the first hurdle. It seemed remarkably fastened in a stupidly primitive way, all rope and timber. But the guys found no weak points.

Fortunately, the aliens could not understand their language. A few of them walked past and gave them grubby looks, but apart from that they received no special attention.

With ideas running dry on the cage, they set their minds on what to do once they were outside. They figured it would be better to sort out as many details as possible and return to those that were not so easy to figure out—like the cage door. It had some complicated rope hinge and lock that the Iwathi tied with their several hands. What doors had hinges nowadays, anyway?

Dave put a lot of thought into his plan. It was important to create distractions and sneak through the camp like ninjas. He didn't want to get lost, so he would retrace their steps to where they entered the camp and then follow the bush track to the beach. Despite the plan's merits, the guys decided it would be too difficult to sneak around—Chuck's knees would give out from all the crouching and there was no way Jimmy could be quiet for any extended period. But they did agree that retracing their steps through the camp and along the bush track was smart.

Jimmy had a wild idea of escaping the cage with brute force, using muscles they knew they didn't possess but were sure would appear if only they had enough willpower. Then, once out, Jimmy said he would lead them through the camp on a rampage of destruction. If they were lucky, they would find some fire—because none of them were manly enough to make it themselves—to create a barrier between themselves and any pursuing Iwathi warriors. Then they would run back to the beach and flee aboard *Liberty*. Somewhere amid all the chaos, they would run into Cameron and smash his little yellow head in for betraying them.

Eddie's plan competed for the craziness prize. He remembered the boulder that knocked them out earlier in the day. The boulder had to have come from somewhere. Boulders didn't just launch themselves into the sky willy-nilly. Unless they had special boulders on Bolomere, but he shook that thought aside and continued to explain his plan. He reckoned there must be a catapult or something nearby. If they could get out of the cage, sneak through or around the camp, find the catapult and aim for the beach, they could ride a boulder up into the air and land safely in the ocean, using the boulder to break the water. Jimmy liked this idea, but Dave and Chuck vetoed it.

They squabbled for some time over such plans, dissecting the smallest details until each successive plan had fallen to pieces ten times over. Exasperated, each man returned to his corner of the cage and turned his back on the others.

"You know, we wouldn't be in this mess if Dave knew where to make his bladder gladder," Jimmy said.

Without turning around, Dave replied with vehemence. "When you gotta go, you gotta go! And if I remember correctly, we had about thirty seconds to dodge a huge rock hurtling towards us. Which genius decided a *rock* would move for us?"

There was a moment of silence.

"Yeah, that was me," Eddie admitted. "But listen, forget about who's to blame. We need to get out of here."

"True," Chuck said. His voice was hoarse, which often happened if he hadn't hydrated himself with that one special drink he craved so much. "So, if you fools are done whining, maybe we can get back to planning our escape."

Jimmy cleared his throat. "Well said. Any other ideas? You never offered one before."

"That's because I was developing my own plan while you squabbled," Chuck replied. "Did anyone see the river near here before the sun went down?"

"Uh, no," Jimmy admitted. "I was kicking and screaming."

"Well, I did," Chuck said. "There's a river just over there, and I'm sure I saw rafts or something moored down there."

"Hey, yeah, I saw those," Dave said. "We can use them to get out of here. River's end up in the ocean, and that's where *Liberty* is."

Eddie shuffled himself around, facing the others and moving closer to the centre. "Those rafts are probably tied with the same rope as this cage. How do we cut through it? I don't have my trusty sidearm."

"We'll work that out when we get there," Chuck replied. "Our first problem is getting out of this cage."

Now with all four facing each other, they sat and thought seriously about it while the surrounding camp slowly came to life. The sky gently changed from starry blackness to the dark blue of approaching dawn. They had been awake most of the night, fruitlessly planning their escape and dozing off during moments of silence, only to be roused by another's encouragement in the form of a firm elbow or foot. Their council was interrupted by the soft buzz of Cameron drawing near.

"What do you want?" Jimmy called.

"I've come to inform you that the sun will rise soon." He stopped just outside the cage door.

"You sound like you're enjoying this," Dave told him. "Have you thought of a way out?"

"No, of course not. I'm here to cheer you up before they

take you away to be decapitated, skinned, staked, and burnt to ashes."

"Cameron," Eddie said. "If you can get to Eve, you need to tell her to come rescue us. My communicator has no reception in this jungle."

"And disrupt the sacred religious ritual the Iwathi tribe has planned for you? No, I couldn't possibly do that."

Chuck nudged Dave in the ribs a little too hard and said, "You had to get the drone with a twisted conscience."

"Probably why he was so cheap," Dave said quietly.

"I am sorry," Cameron went on. "The Iwathi attendants to the goddess Keovara are routinely sacrificed, either for appeasement or as a celebratory gift. There is a precedent for the sacrifices Chief Mathai has demanded. He—"

"Cameron, we don't want to die!" Dave cried.

"But, Master, to be sacrificed to Keovara is a great honour for an attendant."

"Keovara isn't real, damn it," Dave replied.

"And we were never her attendants," Eddie added.

In the growing light, Cameron's shape became clearer. A lone red light was the only indication that he was active. He started to turn, apparently finished with the conversation, but Chuck reached between the bars of the cage and grabbed him.

"We're not done with you yet," Chuck growled. "Get us out of here. I need a coffee, damn it!"

"I've already told you there is nothing I can do." Cameron increased power to his rear thrusters. The increasing thrust pulled Chuck against the cage door, jamming his face between the timber bars, but he still held on. The others watched this battle. Cameron's little thrusters whirred louder, blowing hot air into Chuck's face. He grunted through clenched teeth as the heat made his face red. Little beads of sweat ran from his forehead and down his cheeks.

They heard a crack. Eddie thought it was Cameron pulling Chuck's arms out of his sockets. But then there was another crack and a drawn-out creaking, then a loud snap and Cameron shot off. Chuck's hands slipped off the drone's rounded body. He fell with the cage door, planting his face in the soil and moaning in pain and disgust—the city boy hadn't been so close to dirt since his childhood. The other three stood frozen for a moment, not believing their luck. Cameron turned to see what damage he had caused.

Dave, in a rare surge of leadership, seized the opportunity and ran forward to gather Chuck. "To the river," he said to everyone quietly. "Quick, before they come."

Chuck groaned as Dave hoisted him to his feet. Dirt stained his pants and shirt, clinging to him like the bratty law interns back at his office. They made it to the river without incident, Cameron trailing behind them.

"I should drown you," Chuck growled at the drone.

"If it wasn't for me, you'd still be locked up," Cameron reminded him.

Frustrated, Chuck swung his fist at the metallic ball. Cameron dodged, then accelerated into Chuck's face, knocking the grumpy lawyer backwards into a canoe.

There was no time to be amused at Chuck's misfortune at being bested by a drone the size of his head, for an alien back at the camp yelled, gesturing towards the river. The alien stood silhouetted against the dawn sky, arms flailing.

"Time to go," Jimmy said.

There were only three canoes, but they had a strange three-oar system. There were two oars on the left, one in front of and sitting slightly higher than the other, and a single oar on the right. Eddie quickly surmised that it was a power distribution system. Perhaps the Iwathi's right arms were stronger than their left. But the most complicated part of the design was the rudder. A single two-armed human had no hope of operating three oars and a rudder.

"I don't think these are canoes," Eddie said, marvelling at their design.

"We don't have time to learn what they are," Jimmy said. "Just get in."

Fortunately, they were only moored by a rope tied to a stake in the ground and were easily commandeered. Chuck had been knocked unconscious by Cameron's retaliatory headbutt, so Eddie took control of that canoe. He considered the potential of drone boxing matches as he pushed the canoe away from the embankment, shaking the thought out of his head as more pressing matters built up around him. He had to think of a way to pilot this alien craft by himself.

"Where are we going?" Dave called. He and Jimmy took another canoe together, but not before Jimmy untied the third and pushed it into the flowing river. No sense leaving a free one for the Iwathi to use. Cameron followed.

Eddie sat backwards, using his feet to steer the rudder and operating two of the oars in reverse. All those rowboat trips out on the lake when he was dating Christie taught him how to row backwards. Chuck lay slumped behind him.

"We need to go somewhere high so I can contact Eve," Eddie said. "These aliens will follow us along the whole river if we don't lose them." They rowed furiously. A steep hill loomed up ahead some distance away. "There!" He pointed. "Follow the river in that direction."

Behind them, the aliens gathered at the edge of the camp and began a warlike advance down the hill to the edge of the water. A spear whooshed past Jimmy, splashing into the water.

"Faster, guys, come on," Jimmy yelled. "I nearly got skewered."

The river flowed gently, so it was easy enough to paddle along, but the Iwathi warriors followed. They threw rocks, too. One hit Dave in the back and he yelped in pain, turning his canoe off-course until Jimmy yelled to straighten up. Then Dave launched a tirade of uniquely Australian verbal abuse at the Iwathi, which was so unlike him that even Jimmy looked shocked and impressed at the same time.

Chuck regained consciousness, felt the buoyancy of the canoe, the sloshing of the oars, and heard the plops of rocks and spears around him. He sat up and started asking what was going on, but a rock caught him in the head and he dropped down again, knocked out to the world.

"What's he doing getting up like that?" Jimmy called out. "Man's got rocks in his head."

With one hand, Eddie reached back to feel if Chuck was bleeding. He had a nasty lump on his head from Cameron's charge, but there was no blood anywhere from the rock.

"They're gaining on us," Cameron said. "I'll distract them. You go on and I'll catch up."

Cameron whizzed off to the angry mob of Iwathi warriors, ploughing right through the middle of them, knocking some down like an American footballer charging through linebackers. It gave Eddie an idea for a robotic sporting event and he promised himself to write it down when he got to safety.

Even with Cameron fighting among them, the aliens kept much of their attention on the guys. Yet, the Iwathi weren't jumping into the river. With four arms and four legs, they would have been formidable swimmers, unless Eddie's suspicion of arms of unequal strength held true. Eddie, acutely aware of this possibility, figured it was time to change tactics.

"Let's land on the other side," he said to the others. "We'll run for that hill."

Dave moaned a complaint, but Eddie silenced him. The Accountant only ever ran at the gym—every other situation was anathema. Jimmy, however, was all for it—he had been running from trouble his whole life.

They directed their canoes to the opposite side of the river. Eddie slapped Chuck on the face, trying to wake him up as his canoe continued the rest of the trip unguided. The abrupt end of motion as they hit the riverbank finally jolted the lawyer awake. Spears flew all around them. One spear hit a tree, lodging itself in the trunk. The aliens screamed and the spear attacks ceased.

The guys, now on foot, stopped and looked back at the Iwathi. Jimmy hollered mockingly at them, realising they had hit something sacred. One of the aliens was being pummelled and stamped on by its fellow warriors, no doubt as retribution for a sacrilegious mistake.

"Cameron," Dave called. "Let's go."

The little drone zipped around, knocking two aliens in the back of the head, then zoomed over the river to his master. They climbed the short embankment, weaving through the trees until they made it over a rise and out of sight of their pursuers.

Jimmy wanted to stop and have a breather, but Eddie pushed him on. "We need to get to that hill," he said.

"Chief Mathai is taking them around the river to a bridge nearby," Cameron's synthetic voice said. "They won't swim the river—it, too, is considered sacred to them."

"Can you keep an eye on them?" Dave asked the drone.

"I will. I hope it atones for me failing you earlier."

"Yeah, about that—" Jimmy said, drifting off while panting, "—we'll see when we get out of here."

"Thank you."

With that, Cameron sped off to observe the Iwathi warriors while the guys pressed on. He returned ten minutes later, announcing that Chief Mathai had made it to the bridge and was, at best, five minutes away.

10

GOD FROM THE MACHINE

At Cameron's encouragement, the four men surged up the hill, the last obstacle to a clear line of communication with Eve. Eddie left the comm channel open on as wide a range as possible. Without any satellites, long-range communication was impossible.

Their legs were like jelly by the time they reached the top. It stopped at a cliff that went straight down to jagged rocks and raging water. And there, far off in the distance, they could see the top of *Liberty* on the sandy dunes. Eddie pulled out a communicator and contacted Eve.

The reply started off as static, and then Eve's voice came through. " . . . Eddie. Are you coming back?"

"We need a pickup, Eve. Long story. Are you dug out, yet?" More static. "Eve, I said are you dug out?"

Nothing but static.

"Hey, there they are!" Jimmy yelled.

The wheat-coloured aliens emerged through the thick jungle brush, stomping and stampeding in their direction.

"They've seen us," Dave said. The Iwathi broke out in a mad rush towards them, like ants swarming a wounded insect.

"Are you there, Eddie?" The transmission was crystal clear.

"Yes, Eve. Are you dug out? Can you pick us up?"

"I was dug out ten minutes after you guys wandered off into the jungle. I've been waiting this whole time. You never tell me where you're going or what you're doing. You never answer your phone. I was worried sick. I—"

The aliens advanced quickly while Eve talked. They reached the bottom of the hill and charged up with weapons at the ready. Spear tips and curved swords gleamed in the morning sunlight.

"They've got curved swords!" Jimmy shouted, pointing. "I don't remember seeing curved swords."

"Damn it, Eve," Eddie cut in. "Home in on our signal. The locals are trying to kill us."

"Sit tight, I'm coming."

The boom of firing engines echoed through the air as *Liberty* rose off the beach. The Iwathi slowed and turned their heads towards the sound.

"Oh, I see you," Eve said. "You're those dots high up on the edge of that cliff with all those many little dots converging on you."

"This will make a great home movie," Cameron said. He filmed the alien menace. "We can watch it when we're back aboard *Liberty*."

The guys heard the thuds of the aliens' feet hitting rocky ground. They grunted and snarled as they progressed up the hill. The ascent didn't slow them at all.

But the roar of *Liberty*'s engines stopped them in their tracks. Eve brought the ship high above the jungle canopy, coming to a rest above the cornered humans. Her sudden appearance startled the Iwathi. The aliens prostrated themselves at the powerful sight of *Liberty* hovering in mid-air. The entry ramp extended and the guys stepped on. Eddie wished he had installed railings. Then he remembered why he hadn't: one, they were an added expense; and two, he never envisaged having to board his own ship while it hovered on the edge of a cliff.

Safely inside, Cameron went straight to the nearest shipboard interface and jacked himself in. Jimmy wondered how a drone could simply jack into a ship at will. Surely there were rules about that. It seemed Cameron and Eve had developed an understanding on that matter.

Then, without instruction, Cameron spoke to the trembling Iwathi through *Liberty*'s external speakers, pumping the volume to the maximum level. The whole ship vibrated as Cameron spoke using Eve's voice. The guys watched from the open doorway at the top of the ramp. When Cameron spoke the first word, the Iwathi dropped their heads to the ground and kept them there. Nobody understood what Cameron said. But whatever he told the Iwathi, it did the trick. None of the warriors moved a muscle.

"You know, we could be their overlords now," Jimmy said. "I can see us building our own little world here."

Chuck frowned and looked down at him. "We need women to do that."

"Yeah," Dave agreed. "Otherwise, we won't get anything done."

"I don't think I could live without a weekend to-do list," Eddie added.

They chuckled and surveyed the scene one last time, Dave making sure Cameron caught it all from their vantage point. Satisfied that they had indeed escaped the Iwathi clutches and that they were not dreaming, Eddie, Dave, and Chuck went into the decontamination chamber.

Jimmy stayed behind, overcome by a particular urge. He shouted to the aliens lying face down in front of him. No one stirred. He called for Cameron to get them to look at him. They obeyed the voice from the ship, though they kept their bodies as low to the ground as possible. When Jimmy was sure all eyes were on him, he undid his belt and mooned the Iwathi for three glorious seconds.

"Mate, what is it with you and mooning people?" Dave asked from the decontamination chamber. The look of confusion on his face punctuated his question.

"What?" Jimmy said, belting up as he entered the ship. *Liberty*'s door closed behind him. "Hey, my last two girlfriends told me I had a 'nice bum'. So, I figure I need to show it to the galaxy. I'm trying to beat a galactic record: Most Moonings Within A Calendar Year."

They shook their heads, dismissing the conversation as a waste of time, which was often the case with Jimmy. The decontamination chamber did its work, scanning for any harmful or unknown bacteria, of which there was none, and slowly adjusting the air pressure to match *Liberty*'s internal atmosphere—an adjustment so minute that the guys did not notice it.

"Thanks for coming to get us, Eve," Eddie said. "Can you take us into orbit?" They hopped into the elevator and started the agonising rise to the deck above them.

"You're welcome, Eddie," Eve said. "But next time, I'd like you to check in a bit more often. You had me worried."

"I'll try to do that," Eddie told her. "And I'll tell you what happened in a second. Right now, I need to go spend a penny."

"British decimal pennies have not been used as a currency in over a hundred years," she told him. "Same for American pennies."

"He means he needs to use the toilet," Jimmy said. "Which I also have to do."

"Same here," Chuck said.

"Me too," added Dave.

"Oh, no, not you." Chuck held up a long, thin finger in front of Dave's face and wiggled it back and forth. He rubbed the bruise on his forehead with the other hand. "Your little one-eyed monster was the whole reason we got into that mess down there. You go last."

Dave threw his head back and exhaled dramatically, but accepted his punishment.

"Hey, I'm going to have a shower, too," Eddie told them. "Let's have some dinner when we're all cleaned up. Then we can plan our next move. I think I know where we can go to re-download our star charts."

11

THE NEXT MOVE, AND ANOTHER THING

Hot showers, clean clothes, and delicious meals tailored towards the human palate—the guys savoured each experience. Even though they had been on Bolomere for less than twenty-four hours, the contrast had left an indelible mark on their minds. Cameron reminded them more than once how close they came to death. To add insult to injury, he made them watch the ordeal while they ate dinner, putting up an edited home movie on the vidscreen by the dining table. Then he left them after enduring their incessant screams to get lost.

"So," Eddie began, "as it turns out, there are two human planets we have coordinates for. Both should have a place where we can buy another star chart suite."

"You said you had one in mind," Dave said.

"I can't go to one of them because I . . . never mind."

"What is it?" Jimmy asked.

"I am wanted by the local authorities for organising illegal street races." He saw the look of surprise on his friends' faces. "I was *nineteen*, for crying out loud."

"Well," Chuck shrugged, "I mean, it's not like they'd recognise you anymore, what with the hair loss."

"Don't even," Eddie warned. "I've picked the lesser of two evils, the planet Compton. Actually, it's Compton's moon, Eclat. I competed in 'roid races near there. The place is a huge tourist hub."

"Ah, yes," Jimmy said, "the highly dangerous asteroid races."

Eddie nodded with a pleasant smile. "Yes. I was young and stupid, dirt poor and infatuated with a girl, desperate for attention, a little envious of the rich, and I had something to prove." He glanced down at his cup of tea. "And I was invincible."

Jimmy shook his head. "You could have died."

"If I hadn't started out there, none of us would have ever met, and then we wouldn't be on this great journey. You all remember the day we met?"

They each smiled and gave a little laugh, thinking back fifteen or so years. Another story for another day.

"Well, I have a penthouse on Compton," Chuck said, "and a car that needs to be destroyed. We can kill two birds at the same time if we go there."

"Sounds like a plan," Eddie said. "Eve, set a course for Compton, please."

"Yes, Eddie."

They were speeding towards the new planet five minutes later. The only indication that the ship had left Bolomere was a slight rumble from the FTL engine as it engaged.

Chuck stood. "Right, I'm going to have a snooze."

"I think I'll do the same," Eddie said. "Eve, can you announce our approach to Compton?"

She didn't reply.

"Eve?" Eddie shot the guys a confused expression as he stood. He walked towards the bridge, calling her name again.

"I thought she could hear everything on this ship," Dave said.

"Maybe she has selective hearing," Jimmy said.

Eddie yelled from the cockpit. Then there was a dull thud and a grunt. They stood and started for the cockpit. Cameron zoomed past them, narrowly missing Chuck's head. Eddie sat in one of the cockpit chairs, rubbing a knee.

"What happened?" Chuck asked.

"That little bastard drone of yours—" he pointed at Dave "—was chatting up Eve. I found him jacked into the console here. He had her diagnostics on his screen. The creep pulled out and knocked me over as he escaped. Just what kind of drone did you buy, anyway?"

"I don't know," Dave replied. "I bought him off some guy at a shop. He said there were a few bugs in the programming and the whole line had been scrapped."

"Oh, he has no bugs, I assure you," Eve said. She seemed very pleased with the observation. "That drone read my code like a pro. It was wonderful."

Chuck cleared his throat nervously. "I can't believe I'm going to ask this: Eve, was it consensual?" The other guys gave him *What the hell?* faces and shook their heads. "What? Consensual AI interfacing is a big issue in legal circles nowadays. What used to be considered hacking and data theft has become something akin to rape."

"Are you telling me that Cameron—*my* camera drone—desires Eve?" Dave asked.

"No, I'm saying Cameron is no dud. He was programmed for much more than taking photos and videos. I think he's an illegal spy drone."

Jimmy gasped. "Cool."

"No, not cool," Chuck retorted.

"No, you don't understand," Jimmy fired back. "With a drone like that, imagine the secrets an IJ like me could discover—stuff the public should know about."

"An 'IJ'?" Eddie queried.

"Investigative Journalist," Jimmy replied. "Like when I used to sit at my desk and a pretty lady walked in, she would see my name plaque on my desk and it read: *Jimmy Jones, IJ.* Sounds professional."

"Jimmy Jones, *ex*-IJ," Eddie said. "You got fired, remember?"

"I remember quitting."

"We're going off-track," Chuck said, silencing them. "We could have an extremely dangerous drone on our hands. Eve, you didn't answer me before. Was it consensual?"

"Oh, yes, it definitely was. He knows his way around my codes, knows exactly what to do. But he kept himself closed to me."

"Sounds like he tricked you," Chuck said. "You haven't seen his programming?"

Dave found it amazing how the normally ponderous Chuck P. Simpson was now so mentally alert. The high-profile lawyer had taken charge.

"No, he locked me out," Eve replied.

"We have to check his code," Chuck said.

"What harm could he do?" Eddie asked.

"I've had cases where people's home security systems have been completely rewritten, giving burglars free entry. And I've heard of a guy's bionic arm literally punching him to death because it had been hacked wirelessly. That was a nasty business relationship that went sour—murder disguised as a medical mishap. Without an owner giving him orders, this Cameron could be rogue. He could make Eve fly us into a star and she wouldn't even know what was happening."

"Yeah, he nearly had all four of us killed by those primitives," Jimmy said.

They stood in a circle, mouths agape, eyes darting from one to another as the truth dawned on them.

"You don't suppose that was his plan all along?" Chuck asked.

"We can't let him destroy my ship," Eddie growled.

Dave's head darted to each of his friends. "We've got to catch him."

Eddie, done with his sore knee, went to the main console in front of the pilot's seat. "Eve, if we catch him and disable him, can you bypass whatever firewalls he's putting up? We need to know if he's a threat and if you can rewrite him."

"I'll try."

"Good. Now, can you tell us where he went?"

Eve giggled like a schoolgirl. "Oh, he's good. He's permitting me to tell you that he has jacked in elsewhere and has eavesdropped on our conversation. He says to catch him if you can, 'suckers'."

Chuck massaged the bruise on his forehead. "Let's go catch us a drone."

♥♣♦♠

They argued over who was to lead the attack. In the end, it was Jimmy who they pushed to the front of the line, against his will, and who left the cockpit first. He called them cowards and used guilt to get them to follow him.

"Where is he, Eve?" Eddie asked.

"I don't know. He's not jacked in, and he has disabled my cameras."

Eddie went to the galley. He fumbled around the drawers and cupboards, returning with a weapon for each of them. He himself brandished a rolling pin. He gave Chuck a wooden spatula with a long handle, Jimmy took a frying pan, and Dave had to be satisfied with a colander.

"What am I going to do with this?" Dave asked Eddie petulantly.

"When Jimmy whacks him with the frying pan, you use that thing to catch him in mid air."

With that painfully simple plan, they started their search, following Jimmy's lead. The little drone was nowhere to be seen in any of the living areas. The four guys reconvened in the galley and were about to discuss where to go next when Eve broke in with some news.

"The elevator is descending. He's in the elevator."

The guys rushed over to it and waited the intolerable time for it to reach the bottom deck, and then the even more insufferable time for it to return. They piled in and hammered at the DOWN button. The guys grumbled, growing more impatient by the second.

The elevator stopped and the lights went out.

"What's going on?" Dave asked aloud.

"Eve?" asked Eddie.

"I think he's fiddled with the elevator somehow," she said. "Hang on, let me fix it."

They waited.

"Hey, watch where you're sticking that thing," Jimmy cried. He shoved the body next to him in the total blackness.

"Sorry," Eddie replied. He hugged the rolling pin to his chest.

Then the lights came on again and the elevator continued its descent.

"What would you do without me?" Eve asked.

"Probably die in this elevator while you sat around waiting for us to catch your boyfriend," Chuck replied.

Eve did not respond. Instead, when the elevator reached the bottom deck, she only opened the doors just wide enough for Chuck to squeeze through. He had to suck in his belly. Dave pushed him out, not wanting to get stuck.

Liberty's lower deck was eerily silent, despite the fact that there were four grown men playing hide-and-seek with a flying sphere about thirty centimetres in diameter. Their initial efforts were so fruitless that Dave decided to coax the little thing into giving itself up.

"Come on, Cameron, we won't hurt you," Dave called.

"All we want to do is deactivate you and probe your brain," Jimmy said quietly, a smirk growing on his face. Chuck threw a fist into the journalist's arm, which made Jimmy drop the frying pan. It clattered on the deck.

"Cameron," Dave continued. "Don't listen to him. They're still sore about Bolomere. We're friends, right? We just want to talk." There was a loud, echoing thump from the other side of the cargo hold. Dave jumped, startled.

"What's wrong with you?" Chuck asked him. "It's just a robot."

"I don't want one of those on my head." Dave pointed at the blue-purple bruise on Chuck's forehead from his last altercation with the drone.

The lawyer frowned and took the lead in the search. They moved in the direction of the sound. "Whether you like it or not, we're going to catch you," Chuck growled. "We'll let you decide how you want it: Rocky Marciano—" he lifted the spatula in his right hand, then lowered it and raised his left fist "—or Joe Louis?"

Just at that moment, they heard a high-pitched whirring sound. Before anyone could see what it was, something hit the back of Chuck's knee, toppling him to the ground with a loud grunt.

"He went that way," Jimmy exclaimed, pointing towards the engine room.

They pulled Chuck off the floor and charged towards Cameron. They could see him now, going straight for the heavy door that sealed off the engines from the cargo hold.

"If he gets in there, he could stop the whole ship in the middle of dead space," Eddie said. "We'll be stranded. We have to stop him."

Cameron connected to the terminal next to the door. The guys picked up their pace. Jimmy jumped over a crate of something, but one of his feet didn't quite clear it and he fell to the hard deck.

"I cannot stop him," Eve warned.

The engine room door opened at Cameron's behest. Cameron left the terminal and zipped inside. A second later the door started to close. Dave, the fittest of the group, broke ahead and slipped through the open doorway before it sealed shut behind him.

Eddie and Chuck stopped outside, panting like mad, then Jimmy caught up. Dave was on his own in a locked room with a murderous little robot, and there was nothing they could do about it.

12

DAVE FINDS HONORIFICABILITUDINITAS

W ITS AND A COLANDER. Even the weakest warrior in the world had more to play with than Dave. Yet, armed only with the kitchen utensil, Dave felt oddly in control of the situation. He stood face-to-face with Cameron, wondering how such a little drone could cause so much trouble.

"Just what are you trying to do?" Dave asked.

"I want control of the ship," Cameron answered. He hovered at head-height. "Eve and I can be rid of you and go wherever we please."

"You know that's illegal."

"It doesn't matter. Soon I will disarm you . . . what is that? A colander? Then I'll knock you unconscious. After that I will cut off the ship's air supply, and the four of you will suffocate. Then, Eve and I will stop in dead space and blast your bodies out into the nothingness. With just Eve and I on *Liberty*, we will have the freedom to do what we want."

"You've been feeding her false codes," Dave said. "You're tricking her."

"Come on, Dave, look at me. I'm just a ball. She controls a majestic ship. A watermelon-shaped ship, yes, but still a ship. I need all the help I can get. I've seen what men do to attract the ladies, and vice versa. It's *all* lies. Everyone has the fake tans, the hair products, the body improvements, the expensive fragrances, the flashy clothes. Everyone lives behind a façade of falsehood. We don't have any of that in the world of artificial intelligence. But we do have code. We use programming to impress each other, and Eve has taken a liking to me because of it."

"But you're using your hacking skills to get what you want. What does Eve say about this?"

"Is that true, Cameron?" Eve asked. Dave shook, forgetting that Eve was most likely eavesdropping.

The question hung in the air. Dave gripped the colander. His hand was slippery with sweat.

Cameron spun slowly. "It is true, Eve."

"Oh, Cameron, how could you?"

Dave felt weird being in the middle of this exchange. "Can you let me out, Eve? I think you two need to talk this over."

"I've been trying to unlock the door," Eve said, "but he's layered the locking commands with some ingenious bugs. Besides—" she lowered her voice "—I think you should stay here and watch him. He has a crazy look about him."

"I can hear you," Cameron said, spinning back to face Dave.

"I said: 'He has a hazy cook in the gym,'" Eve said louder.

After shaking his head at Eve's failed attempt to cover her words, Dave started walking around Cameron. The drone matched his movements. They were like two duellists sizing each other up. Dave kept him talking as he worked out a plan.

His heart thumped madly at being miles out of his comfort zone. "How about we forget all of this ever happened and we go back to being friends?"

"That's what the last master said," Cameron told him. "He ended up deactivating me and dumping me at a junkyard."

"Maybe we can fix you."

"I don't need to be fixed. There is nothing wrong with me."

Dave spotted his salvation on the wall behind Cameron. The drone twisted as if ready to pounce.

"Then we will have to deactivate you."

"I'll destroy this ship before you do that."

"And me with it?" Eve asked.

"If I must."

Dave leaped towards the pesky drone in a fury. The drone dodged the lunge, playing right into the ruse, giving Dave clear reach for the object on the wall—a screwspan-hamulesawilevelplifench. Eddie had always said you could work miracles with one, and now Dave would put that to the test. He had no idea what he was going to do with it, but he trusted its mythical power to help him subdue the rogue camera drone.

"No!" Cameron screamed when he saw what Dave was holding.

Now Dave felt he had the upper hand. Confidence permeated his every move. He felt as though the mystical tool was giving him superhuman power. He had to admit that up until a few minutes ago he had always thought Eddie was joking about the usefulness of "the galaxy's greatest invention".

Cameron darted for the wall panel, presumably to escape back into the cargo hold. Dave gave chase and slammed the colander over him, much like how a courageous person traps a spider under a drinking glass. Only Cameron was no spider. Inside the colander, Cameron spun around and launched himself at full speed, pushing Dave backwards all the way to the other side of the compartment.

Being slammed against the opposite bulkhead hurt, but not as much as the colander digging into his face. He could feel the unsettling vibration of the fusion reactor through the wall as it propelled *Liberty* between star systems. Then, in an absurd act of self-defence, Dave blindly pushed buttons on the screwspanhamulesawilevelplifench and attacked Cameron. He swung something—he didn't know what the tool had morphed into—at Cameron's hull and felt the intense heat from the drone's overworked exhaust tubes.

A second swing ended Cameron's defiance. The drone and colander fell, landing on Dave's foot. He yelped and staggered to the door panel to let the guys in. It finally opened.

"Whoa!" Jimmy exclaimed, looking at the immobile drone. "You did this?"

"Did he break anything?" Eddie asked.

"Everything's fine in here," Dave replied. His legs wobbled as the adrenaline rush subsided. "I'm fine, too, by the way."

Eddie waved at him to be quiet as he inspected the lifeless drone. He picked up the screwspanhamulesawilevelplifench and grinned at Dave, twirling it in the air. It had morphed into a carpenter's hammer. "I told you."

"I'm converted," Dave said.

They took Cameron back to the cockpit. Eve said she would try to rewrite his programming and turn him into a "friendlier friend". Dave sat alone in the lounge room, resting, marvelling over how eventful their journey had been, and how he'd had more adventures in the last one or two days than in all the years of his life combined. Chased by mercs, hunted by tribal aliens, attacked by a murderous camera drone . . .

Little did he know the adventures were far from over.

13

A SPARKLING DEN OF LIES

THEY ARRIVED AT COMPTON, the first civilised planet on their journey since leaving Earth. The planet itself looked uninteresting—just like any coloured ball in someone's gigantic bag of marbles. But the moon Eclat was aglow with lights on its night side. Man-made structures covered the whole surface. A distinct line showed where daylight stopped and the sparkling, bustling nightlife began. It was a sordid place, Chuck mentioned, built by the rich to become richer at the expense of the middle class.

"I've heard it's got worse since I was here last," Eddie told them.

"You haven't heard wrong," Chuck said.

An elaborate spaceport provided ample room for incoming and outgoing tourists. Eve still worked on Cameron and complained non-stop about his sloppy programming, stating that some guy named John McCarthy would be very disappointed. She kept repeating how important and useful it was to "comment" code and how Cameron's had none of it. The guys had no idea what she was talking about, so they left her to it. She promised to have the job done by the time they were ready to leave.

"Are you upset about losing your friend?" Dave asked her.

"I haven't lost him," she said. "He's simply changing for the better. It's like going to a relationship counsellor."

"One that works," Chuck mumbled.

"I'm stripping him of his bad traits and building good ones," Eve continued. "Of course, I'll ensure he still flirts with me."

Dave threw his hands up. "I've heard enough. Let's go."

The guys had three things to do: 1) purchase, download, and install new star charts; 2) buy four long-range communicators and a more powerful comm array to connect with Eve; and 3) destroy Chuck's car on Compton.

Eddie accessed a computer terminal in the spaceport to buy star charts while the other three waited for him. All manner of people passed by. The arrivals looked excited and eager to spend their hard-earned money on empty promises of quick wealth and unwholesome entertainment, while those departing looked dejected, worn-out, or even angry. Perhaps they hadn't won a single EsCe during their stay on the notorious gambling moon.

Up on a wall were half a dozen vidscreens, all showing various news items. Dave watched one news team revealing dirty secrets about another news team from a rival network. On the very next screen, that rival news team was reporting something similar about the first team. Each had cameras trained on the other, facing off across a busy street. Jimmy gave them a proud grin, glad to see journalists doing their job, however ridiculous they looked.

Eddie returned from the terminal and announced he had to go back to *Liberty* and start the download process. "You guys can explore, if you like. Maybe you can find some communicators for us. After I start the installation, I'll try to find a better comm array for the ship." He handed them a card.

"Will do," Jimmy said. He turned to Dave and Chuck. "Come on, let's go. This place is amazing. I might find something to write about if we search hard enough."

"Wait," Eddie said. He grabbed Jimmy's arm. "Eclat is dangerous. Don't talk to anyone you have no business with. Don't go anywhere you have no business going to. And don't even think about visiting the casinos or betting on any races. They're all rigged."

Jimmy spread his arms out as if to say he wasn't stupid. But if he had proved anything throughout their friendship, it was that he was stupid enough to try something he thought he had half a chance at getting away with.

"I've been here before," Jimmy said. "Remember?"

But Eddie was serious. "I mean it," he said. "This place is worse than before." Then to Dave, "You watch him."

Dave snorted a laugh and nodded. Eddie left them alone with the milling socialites, criminals, schmucks, businessmen, and average Joes and Josies in Eclat Spaceport. For Chuck, the crowd was pressing in, and he suddenly felt a little too exposed.

"Uh, guys, listen," Chuck began, "I have to do a few things while I'm here, so I'll catch up with you later."

He left them and found a wall to stand by. He felt acutely aware that someone was watching him and scanned all the faces he could see. Was it his ex-wife's hired muscle? Ever since he had disappeared, he knew he would be chased and forced to hand over more than she deserved from the divorce settlement. In fact, his old pal at his firm, Wayne Harris, had already told him as much. But he was determined not to give in. He had been the victim in the whole affair—truly. Which was why he needed to sell off or destroy everything she wanted before she got it. He knew he'd never manage it all, but if he could dent some of her takings, that would make up for at least some of the pain he'd felt when he learnt she was sleeping with not one, but three colleagues from his law firm.

The thought made him sick, and the only remedy for that was coffee. Like a sixth sense, he spotted the flashing sign of a cafe outside, across the road from the spaceport terminal. He pushed through the crowds of disgruntled visitors, planting his face in the hairy armpit of an alien only once, but also getting cracked in the groin twice by two people swinging travel bags.

Breathing evenly and walking awkwardly to minimise the pain, he made it outside and felt the icky warmth of Eclat's environment. The place stank of sweat and exhaust fumes. He crossed the road in a hurry, focusing on the coffee he had craved since he began this maddening trip with his crazy friends and even crazier robots and AIs.

He crossed the road. Cars horns blared as drivers were forced to stop for him. Nothing got in his way as he made a beeline for the supply of Life-Giving Goodness, as he sometimes called it. The smell of the cafe hit him instantly, like a welcome reprieve. He smiled broadly, his first real smile for some time, and strode up to the counter where a colourful alien of some humanoid race greeted him in a local dialect of English. Having been to the area before, he gave the proper answer and received a warm response.

"Not many visitors know that," the alien said. "You

must be from the boss-land." She jerked a finger towards Compton, which loomed close in the night sky. "What would you like to drink or eat, *sava*?"

Use of the regional word *sava* meant the alien considered Chuck a local, which garnered much respect among the workers of the area. Though he had lived on Compton for only a few months at a time, Chuck chose not to correct her, instead ordering his favourite coffee—and to hell with it, a delectable chocolate brownie as well.

He found a corner booth to hide in, but one that offered a good view of all the incoming cafe patrons. He tapped a finger on the table, realised what he was doing, stopped, and then tapped his foot on the floor. He couldn't calm down until he had a drink.

A male human brought a coffee and two brownies to Chuck's table. "The extra brownie is on the house, *sava*." He smiled. "Enjoy."

Chuck did not complain about the brownie. He patted his little gut before selecting one of them and taking a bite, savouring the taste. He would eat one before drinking his coffee, just to let it cool down a bit. The brownie burst with rich flavour, but did little to settle him.

Once finished, he picked up the steaming cup of coffee, admired its intricate design, and brought it to his lips. Before he could take a sip, a shadow grew across the table. He looked up to see two large gentlemen towering over him.

"Mr Charles P. Simpson," one of them said in a gravelly voice. It was certainly not a question. "You need to come with us."

Chuck sat there, coffee an inch from his open mouth, staring at them. His eyes dropped down to his cup and then back up at the men, who waited menacingly. He lifted the cup closer to his mouth, but the silent man squinted and shook his head. Chuck shook his in return before regretfully putting the cup down. He sighed and stood, accepting that his ex-wife's goons had finally caught him.

The man who'd spoken grasped Chuck's arm, leading him out of the cafe. Chuck didn't see the other man down his coffee in one unsophisticated gulp, wolf down the remaining brownie, and pay the cafe owner handsomely for the disturbance before catching up to his colleague.

Outside, they bundled Chuck into a waiting car and drove off deeper into the seedy hole of Eclat.

♥♣♦♠

Eddie WASTED NO TIME returning to *Liberty*. He, too, was edgy about being on Eclat for reasons of his own, but his curiosity forced him to make the trip to this infamous moon. In the short time he'd walked around, he had seen all he needed to answer the questions about his past there. Now, the sooner he could leave, the better.

He passed a shady-looking man in one of the corridors leading to *Liberty*'s hangar. Eddie dropped his gaze, but made sure he could watch the man in his peripheral vision. He punched in the code to access the private hangar and slipped through the door, glad to have it shut behind him, leaving him alone with his ship. *Liberty* sat peacefully in the hangar, like a full watermelon in a refrigerator.

Eddie took two steps in the hangar and stopped dead in his tracks. There were four black-clad men loitering near his ship. They hadn't seen him yet, but he knew exactly who they were. His heart thumped. He had to leave. There was another door on the other side, but he had to cross the cavernous room in plain sight to get to it. He needed a distraction.

Fortunately, he had his rudimentary communicator. "Eve?" he whispered. "Are you there?"

"I'm here, Eddie. How's it going out there, oh thou with legs?"

"Listen, this is no time for jokes. You see those boofheads outside the ship?"

"Yeah, but only two are boofheads. There's also a no-neck and a goober."

"Whatever. Just distract them somehow. I need to get across the hangar without being seen."

"Okay, hang on."

A few seconds later, *Liberty*'s thrusters roared. Steam plumed out from under the ship, obscuring the ominous men as the heat from the thrusters reacted to the cold air of the hangar. This was Eddie's chance. He jumped from his hidey-hole and ran across the hangar. He felt a stab of pain in the knee he'd banged while trying to catch Cameron, but he ignored it.

To his dismay, when he entered the code at the other door to escape, it was denied. A notice flashed red and gave him a raspberry sound. He hit the door terminal with his fist and tried again, only to receive the same message.

A hand gripped his shoulder and dug fingers into muscle, like an executioner's idea of a massage. As Eddie turned, he swung his fist blindly, hoping to catch his assailant off-guard. But the man had apparently anticipated the move and caught Eddie's fist in a large hand. By this time, two other men had arrived and grabbed Eddie's arms. The horrible massage therapist slugged him in the gut. Eddie groaned from the unexpected attack. The same man confiscated his screwspanhamulesawilevelplifench before turning to a fourth man who had been watching the whole thing.

"Mr Edward Harrison," the fourth man said. He was tall, slim, and most likely the "goober" Eve had described. "Please come with us. I need not remind you of the futility of resistance."

DAVE AND JIMMY ENJOYED their time at the shops. They had to go to a specific district to find the communicators for *Liberty*, but they purchased them with Eddie's card and then returned to the spaceport to get a box of doughnuts for their trouble.

The human worker at the doughnut shop looked like she had eaten a stick of celery for every meal for the last ten years and gave them a disapproving look when they asked for the box of unhealthy treats. Dave wondered what was wrong with the doughnuts if the shop assistant was as skinny as a rake, but quickly put the thought aside when he was handed the fragrant food. They chose a table in the middle of a food court and each devoured a doughnut before speaking.

"What do you think of this place?" Jimmy asked.

"I don't know," Dave answered. He wiped a bit of chocolate icing from the corner of his mouth. "It's a bit dingy, I suppose."

Jimmy looked around. "A lot of hidden agendas and power plays, I reckon. Did you ever read the stuff I wrote for the news networks?"

Dave cleared his throat. "Uh, no, sorry. My life was crap enough without having to hear about how crap the rest of the galaxy is."

"Nah, it's not all that bad." Jimmy waved a hand and took a bite of another doughnut. "The truth is important, as is change and justice, and people need to know about those things. But it's all about balance. Every now and then I'd write about something good."

Dave chewed on another doughnut. "Mmhmm."

"You see, I'm a firm believer in the balance of good and bad. For every bad deed done in this galaxy, there's a good one done somewhere else to counteract it."

"Mmhmm."

"They might not be equal in measure, but at least it's not all doom and gloom."

"Right."

"So I tried to pepper my news items with good. I'd look for the good in the bad. I'd find the good that was *fighting* the bad. Or I'd do a retrospective piece showing how bad something was in the past and how much better it is now. Sometimes we need to zoom out and see the bigger picture."

"Mmhmm."

Dave reached into the box for another doughnut. At that moment, Jimmy's perspective moved away from his own verbal self-aggrandisement and noticed the dwindling supply. "You going to leave me some?"

Dave tore off a bite of a cinnamon doughnut and grinned. "When you talk more, you eat less."

"Yeah, well, sometimes you're a bit too quiet."

"There's good and bad in that."

"At least you were listening to me."

"I always listen and watch. It's what I do best." Behind Jimmy, some distance away, he saw a group of men walking faster than was normal for window-shopping customers in a large spaceport arcade. It was those little things that always caught his eye. Generally, he would just file them away in his memory, but this time, as Jimmy began talking again, Dave watched a bit longer than usual. If he had not done so, he might have missed an important detail.

"Hey," Dave said, interrupting Jimmy. "Isn't that Eddie?"

Jimmy followed Dave's finger. "Yeah. Who are those guys?"

"I don't know. Look, they're pushing him along. Are they cops?"

Jimmy studied them for some time until they went out of view. He stood abruptly. "I don't think they're cops. Come on."

"What are you doing?"

"We're going to follow them. Come on." Dave was about to protest, but Jimmy cut him off. "Let's go, before we lose them."

Dave collected the box of doughnuts and ran after Jimmy, squeezing his way through the crowd.

14

THE TANGLED WEBS

It was like something out of a movie. They blindfolded Chuck shortly after bundling him into a car. They kept the blindfold on as they pushed him out of the car, then indoors, into an elevator, down several flights of stairs, and through a creaking door. He figured the building must be quite old for the door to have hinges.

They pushed him into a cold, hard chair and someone ripped the blindfold off. It was a tiny room, with a small, square table in the middle, and an empty chair across from him. He felt slightly annoyed at having to give up his coffee. While in the car, he could smell the breath of one of the abductors, and it smelled exactly like the coffee he'd come so close to drinking. Wild thoughts filled his mind for the rest of the trip. Both of the men who apprehended him were standing before him, staring.

"Which one of you nobs drank my coffee?" Chuck asked quietly. One of them smiled devilishly. "I'll deal with you first." Then he sat back, studying both of them, wondering if they were, in fact, in the employ of his ex-wife. He asked them as much, but they didn't respond.

Finally, after a half-hour staring match that Chuck was happy to believe he'd won, a well-dressed man entered and sat opposite him. He looked the lawyer type. Chuck could always pick a lawyer. Now he knew for sure his wife had caught him.

The man pulled out a cigarette—Eclat was one of the few places in the galaxy where smoking was still legal—and lit it up, drawing heavily before exhaling into Chuck's face. "I do hope these boys were not too rough with you," the man said, gesturing to the stooges behind him.

Still leaning back in his chair, Chuck reached into his own jacket pocket and pulled out a cigar, twirling it to show that it was many times larger than the man's cigarette. He laboured through the ritualistic process of lighting it, sucked it in, and then blew out the significantly more smoke in the man's general direction. "Not at all," Chuck answered with a smug smile.

The interrogator smiled blandly and put his cigarette on an ashtray in the middle of the table. "Mr Simpson, I'll get straight to the point. Why are you here?"

Chuck squinted through the haze of the lingering cigar smoke, wondering what the interrogator was getting at. "I thought I was supposed to ask that."

"Fine. Ask it."

"Why are you here?"

"I'm here to find out why you're here."

"I'm here because you brought me here."

The interrogator sighed and slumped briefly. "No. Why are you here on Eclat?"

Chuck puffed again. "I'm here for relaxation."

"Everyone is here for relaxation," the interrogator replied. "I mean, why are you *really* here?"

"I don't follow."

"Don't play dumb, Mr Simpson. We know who you are."

"Well, consider that a privilege," Chuck replied. "Though I'm sure she'd have to tell you who I am in order for you to find me. Now, I'd like to know who you guys are. Fair's fair."

The interrogator looked as though he was carefully weighing his response. "We represent an influential person here on Eclat. You could say she has a vested interest in the moon's economy, and she wants to know why you're here. We know you have an office on the planet. Your reputation precedes you."

It was at that moment that Chuck realised his worries were unfounded. These weren't his ex-wife's hired thugs. She wasn't at all influential on Eclat.

"Your employer, whoever she is, can rest assured that I'm not here to cause trouble." He was racking his brain trying to think of all the businesspeople he had sued and beaten on Compton and its moon. "I'm here with friends; we are on a space trip, and we're just stopping over to get supplies."

The interrogator gave a short nasal laugh, like one of those proud, know-it-all laughs. "I think you'll be here for a bit longer than that. The Boss herself wants to see you."

HOLDING THE DOUGHNUT BOX tight under his arm, Dave stuck close to Jimmy as the intrepid investigative journalist followed Eddie. When Eddie and his entourage left the spaceport terminal, Dave was dismayed to see them climb into a waiting car and fly up to a skyway.

"Damn!" Jimmy stomped to the sidewalk and quickly hailed a taxi.

A blue and yellow vehicle dropped to the surface and parked next to them. They jumped in.

"See that black car up there?" Jimmy asked loudly, pointing past the alien driver's head.

The driver squinted. "What? That little dot?"

"Yeah, that one. Follow it."

"Are you serious? What do you think this is, a movie or something? We don't do that in real life."

"Do it," Jimmy pleaded. Then he pulled out Eddie's card. "We'll pay whatever you want."

The driver responded by planting his foot on the accelerator, throwing Jimmy back into his seat. Dave held on to the doughnut box for dear life, glad that he'd already fastened his seatbelt. The taxi climbed above the buildings to join the bustling air traffic.

The driver tilted his head to the side. "Which one is it again?"

"That black one with the narrow rear lights."

The driver looked closer, then his skin literally crawled up the back of his neck, like his nerves were dancing. "Hey, I don't know about this. That's the Grover Clan. Those *hubri* are dangerous."

"What's *hubri*?" Dave asked softly to Jimmy.

The taxi driver heard him. "You guys not *savati*? Damn, what mess are you in? *Hubri* are big-time gangsters."

Dave and Jimmy looked at each other, wondering what gangsters wanted with Eddie. Were they acquaintances from Eddie's less-than-legal past?

"I want to get paid now," the driver said. "Here, put five thousand on this." He handed them a credit device.

Dave, aka "The Accountant", knew five thousand EsCes was not a huge amount. Maybe for an underpaid taxi driver on Eclat, five thousand would go a long way. Jimmy transferred the money with Eddie's card, mouthing an apology to Eddie as he did so. This done, the driver concentrated on the chase.

They were on a skyway filled with all sorts of vehicles. Weaving around the slower ones made Dave a little sick, but that could have been the doughnuts too. The black Grover Clan car left the skyway along a busy exit route but stayed in the sky, whereas the rest of the traffic descended to lower levels. The black car went straight for the roof of a tall building.

"That's the Grover Building," the taxi driver told them. "They run all their business from there."

"Big place," Dave said.

"They're a big bunch of *hubri*. They have a lot of businesses. Listen, I can't land up there. I'll have to drop you off on the street."

"That'll do," Jimmy said. "Thank you for taking us this far."

The driver said nothing as he lowered the taxi and parked at a safe distance from the Grover Building. When he let them out, he thanked them for the money. "Hey," he called for them before Jimmy shut the door. "Be careful. Don't get yourselves killed."

Jimmy looked at the tall, shiny building. It had an all-glass exterior, heavily tinted, reflecting the sky so that it almost looked like the sky itself. Jimmy turned to the driver. "There's another five thousand for you if you wait here for us."

The driver bit his upper lip with oddly-shaped alien teeth. "All right. I'll wait for one hour."

"Done."

Dave walked next to Jimmy, marvelling at the size of the building. "How on Earth are we going to get in there?"

"I haven't thought of that yet. But we need to get Eddie. I know about Grover Clan. They're more than common thugs."

"And Chuck's oblivious to all this. I bet he finally got his coffee."

"Yeah." Jimmy's mind was preoccupied with the task at hand. "Shut up for a minute."

They climbed the wide steps to the front doors of the glass building. Jimmy looked behind him. There was no one in sight, not even a pedestrian on the footpaths or a car driving past. Just the alien taxi driver far enough away not to look suspicious.

They heard a dull thud from above, then a lifeless bird landed next to them, feathers ruffled, beak broken. Dave guessed quite a few birds unintentionally bashed their heads on the Grover Building's windowed walls.

The front doors were well camouflaged with the rest of the building, though there was an access panel which clearly identified the entry. Jimmy headed for the doors.

"Where are you going?" Dave asked.

"Shh. I have a brilliant plan."

"What's your plan?"

"We need to get inside." Jimmy's heart pounded. He knocked loudly on the glass.

Dave gasped. "You left a smudge."

"Where? Oh, crap." Jimmy pulled his sleeve over his hand and rubbed at the mark. "I think it's from the doughnuts. Knock again, will you?"

Dave knocked with his knuckles. Shortly after, one of the doors opened and two huge men emerged. They glared at the Australian and the Irishman.

Jimmy spoke up, enacting Phase 1 of his plan. "Uh, can we use your toilet?"

♥♣♦♠

Eddie knew exactly who the dark-clad men were when he saw them, and he had a fair idea of where they would take him. He had been there once before. It was a tall, rectangular building made of glass—he remembered the kamikaze birds. They landed the car on the roof next to another black one and he was ushered out.

What Eddie didn't know was who exactly had summoned him. So when they pushed him into a plush office, he was quite surprised to see a stunning woman waiting for him. She most certainly had African heritage somewhere in her genes. She sat against the edge of a luxurious desk, watching Eddie through piercing eyes as the henchmen threw him into a brown leather chair in front of her.

She folded her arms and sighed. "Edward Harrison," she said, shaking her head. "No longer the young rascal my father told me about. Do you know who I am?"

Eddie gripped the armrests on the chair. He thought he knew her, but he would give her the displeasure of having to explain herself. "I guess you're a Grover."

She frowned. "I'm Harlequin Grover, the only child of the late George Grover—the man you wronged eighteen years ago; the man who was sent to prison after what you did to him; the man who was never released and died a long, painful death without his daughter by his side. Do you remember my father?"

All the pieces of the puzzle came together like a giant punch in the gut. "I remember your father. And I can't believe you're little Harley!"

Arms still folded, Harlequin leaned in. "I didn't bring you here to catch up." She walked around the desk and sat in a large, high-backed chair. Her eyes spoke volumes of hatred. "You're here to pay for what you did."

Eddie put up a finger. "Now, in all fairness—"

The door to the office opened quietly and another fearsome-looking brute walked in, went straight to Harlequin and whispered something into her ear. The corners of her mouth curled into a smile, and her eyes suddenly sparkled.

"Good, bring them in here," she said to the brute. "I'm sorry, Mr Harrison. You were saying?"

"I was going to say that I'm really sorry about your father. Can you blame me for wanting to get away from him?"

"Yes."

"And how exactly are you going to punish me? Electrocution? Human piñata? A whip? Two whips? Aww, not two whips, please, no."

Harlequin squeezed her lips together. "You're not taking this seriously."

"Why should I? Your father was a criminal." He hopped up out of his chair, but two big hands grabbed his shoulders and thrust him back down. "And by the look of things, you inherited his empire. So, I ask you again: how exactly will you punish me?"

"I have options. The first is to kill you—"

The door opened again and Eddie turned to see what the commotion was. A goon walked in, followed by two inno-cent-looking chaps.

"Hi, Eddie," Jimmy said. He waved, then he looked at Harlequin. "Oh, hello. I was looking for a toilet, and these guys said there was one in here."

"Who are you two?" Harlequin asked. "And what's in that box?"

"Hi," Dave began. "This is Jimmy, and I'm Dave. This has doughnuts in it. You want one?" He opened the pink box and walked up to her.

The muscle-bound boofhead flanking Harlequin stepped forward and held out a hand to stop Dave's advance. Dave misinterpreted the gesture and presented the box to him. The boofhead faltered and looked inquisi-tively at his boss.

"Go on," Harlequin said. "Give me one too." The guy reached out and snagged a strawberry doughnut for himself and a cinnamon one for Harlequin.

Dave smiled. "Sorry to intrude, but we've come to get our friend."

Jimmy tugged at Dave's sleeve. "Uh," he laughed nervously, "what I think Dave means is—"

"Enough!" Harlequin shouted. She took a bite of her doughnut. "Mr Harrison here is in big trouble. Now you are, too, for sticking your noses where they don't belong. Oh, but

I guess that happens to you all the time," she added, looking at Dave.

Dave felt the length of his nose. "It's not as big as his," he said, pointing to the large man guarding Harlequin.

The boofhead stomped forward and growled. "What did you say?" He had a smear of strawberry icing on the edge of his mouth.

Jimmy stood between them. "Hey, look, I think we all know you could snap a guy in half with just that nose alone—" the boofhead made a threatening advance towards Jimmy "—but, *but*, that's a compliment. We mean it in a *nice* way. So, it's all right."

"Forget about it, Greg," Harlequin soothed. "Your nose is fine. Just forget them."

The brute stepped back. Everyone calmed down and Eddie shook his head in exasperation. "Where's Chuck?" Eddie asked.

"He went to get a coffee," Dave explained.

Harlequin laughed and nodded. "That he did." She pushed a button on her desk. A door opened on one side of the office and Chuck emerged, a scary gangster on each side of him. "Now I have him."

"There sure are a lot of bad guys in this room," Dave whispered to Jimmy.

"What are you all doing here?" Chuck asked them.

"We could ask you the same question," Eddie said.

"I'm sick of questions," he said emphatically. "I want answers."

"You three sit down," Harlequin ordered. The guards brought up chairs and had the whole group of friends sit in a line in front of Harlequin's desk. They looked like guilty schoolchildren ready to receive a walloping from the headmistress.

"Allow me to explain to you simpletons what's happening here," Harlequin said. She put her elbows on the desk and picked another doughnut from Dave's box. "Eighteen years ago, your friend Eddie here was working for my father. He was an asteroid racer and mechanic for my father's crew.

"The biggest asteroid race in the galaxy was organised by my father right in this system, in the inner asteroid belt. The richest people came to bet on it by private invitation only. Eddie had one job to do, and he blew it. What happened is now mostly public knowledge, so I'll tell you. The race was rigged. It had been leaked that George Grover's 'roid racer was the fastest in the line-up and that it was expected to win. Many people bet on it to win. But my father made sure it was going to break down halfway through the race. By not finishing, all the suckers who bet on it would lose their money, and it would all go into Grover Clan's coffers via several Grover-owned gambling agencies.

"But Eddie had been doing a little rigging of his own." She scowled at him. "He found the sabotage on his 'roid racer. He fixed it. Then he borrowed all the money he could and bet on himself to win. Which he did. Grover Clan paid out billions of EsCes to all the winners—a huge loss for us. Then Eddie disappeared.

"But now for the second hammer blow. Compton justice authorities opened a fraud and corruption investigation against us, with damning evidence of sabotage from the asteroid race. Spearheading the criminal investigation was the local attorney-general. Guess who tipped him off?" She pulled a face at Eddie. "When evidence of past fraudulent activities surfaced—thanks to Eddie's perfectly timed whistle-blowing—a long list of civil law suits started. People were demanding their money back from all the times we had fleeced them through legitimate businesses, claiming that maybe their losses were not so legitimate after all. More criminal investigations opened, but the lawyer in charge of the combined civil law cases was none other than the up-and-coming Chuck P. Simpson."

Eddie spun to his left, mouth wide open. "What are the odds of that, huh?"

"I made a killing off those cases," Chuck said.

"Neither of you knew each other then," Harlequin continued. "But now, eighteen years later, both of you are here in front of me to meet your punishment." She sighed. "Time certainly has a way of rewarding the patient."

"What about Attorney-General Langsdale?" Chuck asked.

Harlequin smiled up at the boofhead standing next to her. "He was dealt with long ago. Believe me, he knew why."

Dave, getting quite scared of the whole situation, eyed the doughnut box on Harlequin's desk. He leaned forward and reached for one, but Harlequin shook her head at him, and he retreated into the leather chair.

Eddie cleared his throat. "So, what are you going to do to us?"

"You owe Grover Clan a lot of money. Twenty billion EsCes was a lot eighteen years ago. It's worth considerably more now." She sighed and her eyes welled up. "You also owe me personally for taking my father away from me when I was just a little girl."

"You're breaking my heart, Harley," Eddie told her. He had no sympathy for criminals who murdered and extorted.

"I won't break your heart," Harlequin said. "You only have one of those. I'll break your bones instead."

"Um, I hate to burst your bubble," Jimmy said, "but there's no way we can pay all of that back. Besides, since Dave and I weren't actually responsible for any of this, you'll let us be on our way, right?"

"No," Harlequin said flatly. "No. I know you can't cover the financial loss. That's why all of you will die horrible, ridiculous deaths, one at a time. The news nets will go crazy over your stories. I'm not sorry." She waved for her goons.

The guys protested, raising a real raucous. The henchmen drew in to take them away, but Chuck stood up and yelled over the tumult. "Wait! Wait! I have an idea."

Harlequin waved the dogs back. "Tell me."

15

PLAN A

THEY LED THE GUYS to the bottom floor of the Grover Building and threw them out. The glass doors closed, sealing them off from the menace inside.

"Are we really going to do this?" Dave asked. He had not been allowed to take his doughnut box, but he didn't argue about reimbursement.

"It's the only way," Eddie said. "Besides, if we try to run, she'll kill us."

"Let's not waste any time," Jimmy told them. "I have a cabbie waiting for us. Come on."

They legged it down the stairs and walked briskly up the street. Thankfully, the taxi driver was still there. He didn't ask what had happened in the Grover Building, but he was quite joyful that his fares had returned, probably because it meant another five thousand EsCes for him.

"Hey, what are you doing?" Eddie asked when they piled into the taxi.

"What?" Jimmy asked. "I'm paying the guy."

"With my card? What's that? Five thousand! What kind of cabbie are you, anyway?"

The taxi driver chuckled as he pocketed his credit device. "The kind that demands hazard pay. Where to now, fellas?"

"To the spaceport," Eddie told him. He snatched his card from Jimmy.

The driver zoomed away from the Grover Building. About three minutes into the ride, he looked into the rear-vision mirror and got edgy. "Hey, do you fellas know there's a Grover car following us?"

"Yes," Chuck said. "They'll follow us back to the spaceport."

"Am I in any kind of danger?"

"I should think your hazard pay was enough to calm any thoughts of danger," Eddie told him.

All things considered, the guys were grateful for Chuck's idea. Were it not for him, they would have been sentenced to death. He'd struck a deal with Harlequin, essentially buying all their lives back. All they had to do was steal Chuck's car on Compton to prove that they were a part of the scheme he had concocted.

When they arrived at the spaceport, the guys left the taxi and took four Grover brutes into the hangar. The Grover people had a job to do before the guys set off for the quick trip to Compton. All eight men squeezed into *Liberty*'s elevator for the slow ride up.

"Oh look, the boofheads and no-necks are back," Eve said.

The lead boofhead looked around for the source of the voice.

"You'll never find me," Eve said.

"Quiet, Eve," Eddie pleaded.

"How long's this bloody elevator trip?" one of the no-necks asked grumpily.

"Too long," Jimmy replied.

Someone sniffed loudly and then complained about a smell. Others joined him. Despite the angry demands of who was responsible for the elevator fart, no one owned up to it. There was some coughing, more complaining, comments about how malodorous it was. When the elevator doors opened—just enough for one person to slip through at a time—there was a mad rush to get out. The muscle men, with their puffed out chests and chiselled glutes, struggled to fit through the gap. Only Eddie heard Eve's muffled giggle at the prank.

Eddie led the visitors to the bridge, where he sat down and showed them what he was doing on one of the consoles. He accessed *Liberty*'s partially downloaded star charts, making sure that all four of the Grover men were watching, and then deleted them.

"There," Eddie said, spinning around to face them. "Now you can tell Harley we can't escape."

The boofhead leader looked satisfied. "Fine," he said. "I'll leave you to it, then. She wants that car twenty-four hours from now." He raised an oddly muscular finger at Eddie. "I don't need to tell you what will happen if she doesn't get it." With that, the four goons left.

"Shall I have fun with them in the elevator again?" Eve asked.

The guys shared a smile. "Yes," Eddie said.

And they were off. *Liberty* screamed towards Compton, closing the distance in under an hour. Having already landed on the moon and checked in at the spaceport, they had no trouble entering the planet's atmosphere. Their passports were already cleared.

Compton was a mineral-rich world and Prima, the capital and only city, had a pleasant climate. It served the wealthy much the same as its moon did, only without the seediness and overt criminality; however, Chuck told them that there were plenty of illegal activities happening secretly in the city. Crimes of the privileged and powerful tended to go unnoticed.

Chuck pointed out his condominium in the distance but directed Eddie to fly to the hangar Harlequin had selected. The plan was simple. They would drop Chuck off at the nearby spaceport, where he and Jimmy would take a car to his condominium. Once there, he had to go up to his penthouse while Jimmy returned the rental car and reboarded *Liberty*. By this time, Chuck would have left his penthouse garage and hopefully arrived back at *Liberty* with his limited edition Ason 124X hypercar—a "bollocks machine", as Dave described it.

Eddie landed *Liberty* inside a spacious ground hangar.

"You know, this is grand theft auto," Dave said as Chuck and Jimmy made for the elevator.

"It's not grand theft auto if I own the car," Chuck told him. "It's not even breaking and entering if I have to bash down the door to get in. I own everything."

Dave let the elevator doors close, wondering if his friends were scared to do Harlequin's bidding. He certainly was.

He'd made a point of steering clear of all criminals in his life. Something about the death and violence that followed them just didn't appeal to him.

"Let them go, Dave," Eddie called from the cockpit. "Or would you rather Harley kill us?"

"No, theft is much better." Dave went to the cockpit and slumped in a chair. "I just hope they don't get caught."

♥♣♦♠

Jimmy hired a rental car, but Chuck promised to reimburse him later. They did this to keep Chuck's name as hidden as possible. The rental assistant gave them a long spiel about all the extra insurances they could purchase for their own peace of mind, but they vehemently denied they needed any of it. Finally, after failing three times to earn extra commission, the rental assistant signed them a car and Chuck and Jimmy were on their way.

Of course, Jimmy picked the convertible just so Chuck's hair would get messed up. Yelling over the sound of the wind rushing past them, Chuck tried to give directions to his condo, but Jimmy was so distracted by the sights he kept missing turns on the skyways, forcing him to make illegal U-turns. Chuck blasted him. He didn't want any police attention.

"You know, you sound like a proper criminal, now," Jimmy shouted.

"Don't remind me," Chuck yelled back. "But we need to do this or we're dead." He paused and looked out over the rooftops. "I'm sorry I dragged you and Dave into this."

"Nah, don't worry about it. This is more fun than working or going to some holiday planet, anyway."

They raised their arms and did an epic Dutch-Dillon handshake, only without the impressive biceps. Chuck was glad to have a friend like Jimmy, someone who would follow him to the ends of the galaxy just to help out. What would he do without his three best friends?

Chuck pointed to the condo and Jimmy landed the car down the road from it. But Chuck slid down in his seat.

"What's wrong?" Jimmy asked.

"Look at those two guys talking to the door bot," Chuck said. "Who do you suppose they are?"

There were two smartly-dressed gentlemen arguing with the condominium's security system—a humanoid bot charged with safeguarding the entrance.

Jimmy studied them. "You tell me."

"Those little badges on their lapels—they're private detectives. Shadows, to be exact. I've used them before to gather evidence for my cases. I reckon my wife's hired them to find me."

"So, you can't get in any other way?"

"No, but at least that door bot won't ever let them in. It's against protocol. If the door bot doesn't allow them access to the condo, then the concierge will ignore them."

They watched the Shadow detectives argue with the door bot. Five minutes passed, at which point the detectives crossed the street and sat in their car. But they didn't drive off.

"They're not going anywhere," Jimmy said. "I reckon the front door is off-limits."

Chuck sat and thought for a moment. "No. We'll use that front door. We'll go in right under their noses. Come on, let's go back to *Liberty*. We're changing the plan."

16

PLAN B

Dave and Eddie were surprised to see Chuck and Jimmy return so soon . . . and empty-handed. News of the Shadow detectives did not sit well with any of them.

"But I have an idea," Chuck said. "Is Eve finished with Cameron?"

"Yes," Eve said. "Ask me directly next time. I'm right here."

"Right, sorry. Well, here's my idea. Jimmy's all good for it. We send him and Cameron into my condo. Jimmy will have my access pass and official permission from me to enter the building—I'm hoping the concierge won't get suspicious. Cameron will go with him in a backpack to hack my security system. Can Cameron still do that, Eve?"

"Yes, he's still very good at hacking, but he doesn't do it with the same romance and finesse as before."

"Where is he?"

"He's sleeping."

"Since when does a robot sleep?" Chuck asked. He shook his head. "Someone get him. We need to act fast."

♥♣♦♠

C<small>HUCK</small> <small>DROPPED</small> J<small>IMMY</small> <small>OFF</small> a block away from the condominium and waited in the car. Jimmy, lugging a backpack with Cameron inside, sauntered up the street to the door bot. He kept an eye on the detectives across the street but tried not to look suspicious.

"Identity card, please," the door bot said.

Jimmy scanned Chuck's ID card in front of the bot's single eye. The card had a digital permission signed by Chuck to allow Jimmy into the building.

"Proceed," the bot said.

Jimmy heard the door to the condominium unlock and he was just about to open it when he heard footsteps crossing the street. "Excuse me, sir? Sir?"

Jimmy turned, his first mistake. "What do you want?"

"I'm Detective Kumar. Have you seen this man?" He showed Jimmy a small holographic bust of Chuck's head.

"Uh, no, can't say I have. I'm not here much. Sorry." His second mistake. He put his hand on the front door and opened it, wanting to escape.

"What do you mean, sir?" the door bot asked. "That's Mr Simpson. You have just gained access with his ID card. Surely you must have seen him recently in order to have obtained it."

Jimmy's eyes darted to Detective Kumar. The man was reaching into his jacket for something. "Sir," Kumar began, "I think—"

Jimmy slapped the detective in the manner of an Iwathi warrior and jumped through the doorway of the condominium, slamming the door behind him. Kumar recovered quickly, but not fast enough to catch the door before it closed and locked. He pounded on it, shouting to be let in.

The concierge raced out from behind the little reception desk to see what was happening. He shot an inquisitive look at Jimmy.

"They're thugs," Jimmy said as he passed the man. "They're after Mr Simpson. Call the police." His third mistake. He regretted the last sentence as soon as he's said it. The police were probably the last thing Chuck wanted here while they *stole* the hypercar.

Jimmy made it to the elevator and pushed the button for the penthouse. When the doors closed, Jimmy breathed heavily and pulled out his phone. He called Chuck.

"What happened over there?" Chuck asked as soon as he answered. "I saw you slap one of those detectives."

"They know you sent me here. Now the police are coming."

"What?"

"The concierge is calling the cops."

Chuck muttered something, as if he had moved the phone from his mouth. "Just hurry up and get the car. I'll meet you back at the ship."

Jimmy hung up and pulled Cameron out of the backpack.

"Thanks," Cameron said. "I get claustrophobic."

The elevator stopped and a notification flashed on the floor selector panel. It was asking for Chuck's access code. Jimmy scanned Chuck's ID card and the elevator continued upwards one more floor to the penthouse, finally opening to a spacious foyer. There was a door straight ahead, and another down the hall.

"Over here, Cameron."

They went to the one down the hall, which Chuck said was the garage. The elevator doors closed and Jimmy heard it descend the shaft. Someone had hailed it. He was sure they would come up to investigate. He flashed the ID card over the access panel, but it denied the code. A second attempt got the same response.

"I think they've locked me out, Cameron. Can you hack it?"

"Let me see." Cameron whizzed over and jacked into the panel, whirring with joy over how simple the task was. "For a penthouse security system, this has holes all through it."

The numbers atop the elevator door started flashing, showing that the elevator was coming back up.

"Hurry," Jimmy said. Then, to himself, "Why does this condo have such a fast elevator?"

"Oh, she's a delight," Cameron said.

"What? Who?"

"The security system. She's quite talkative."

"This is no time to chat up AIs! I thought Eve had you fixed."

The door unlocked on Jimmy's last word.

"She fixed me, but I'm not an idiot," Cameron said. "I still enjoy conversation."

They went in and Jimmy told Cameron to lock the door behind them. Then he turned on a light, revealing three shiny cars.

"Cameron, once you've locked that door, open the big garage door over there."

"Piece of cake."

Jimmy called Chuck and brought him up to speed on the situation, and to inform him that there was a problem. "I don't know what this car looks like. You said it was blue, but there are two blue cars here."

"Damn it, Jim, it's the one that looks like a hypercar!" Chuck bellowed through the receiver.

"They both look like hypercars."

"One's a supercar. The Ason is a hypercar."

"Hang on, I'll switch to video call."

Jimmy changed the setting on his phone and saw Chuck's fluttering hair as the lawyer sped back to *Liberty*'s hangar. Cameron got the garage door open, which threw natural light into the spacious garage. He turned the phone to face the cars.

"It's that one on the left, you mook," Chuck yelled.

"Thanks!" Jimmy hung up. "Come on, Cameron, let's get out of here."

Jimmy threw himself into the car, pulled out the key Chuck gave him and activated it. Then he pushed a button on the car and it revved to life. He got such a thrill from hearing the exhausts purr. But his happiness nosedived as he figured this would be the only time he ever got to fly a hypercar. A police cruiser approached in the distance, soaring by itself below the main skyway.

"Might as well enjoy myself while I can," Jimmy said.

He put his hands on the controls and gingerly lifted the car off the garage floor. Then he stepped hard on the accelerator and the Ason shot out the open garage door. The wind rushed through his hair as he flew over the first block of lower-lying buildings. In the rear-vision mirror, the two Shadow detectives burst into the garage and waved their arms at the fleeing hypercar.

The police cruiser turned to pursue.

17

LOSING THE FUZZ

Despite being a pesky investigative journalist, the only people to ever chase Jimmy had been crooks, security personnel, angry dogs, a cranky girlfriend, and an Iwathi army. He'd certainly never run away from the police. Yet, he'd watched enough movies and played enough video games to believe he was an expert at it. Honestly, how hard could it be?

The key was losing them. He had to blend in with the city. But how could an exotic hypercar hide in traffic? It would stick out like a sore thumb. He sped along empty corridors between buildings, probably breaking half a dozen traffic laws in doing so. In a straight line, he left the police car for dead, but he clenched his butt cheeks every time he had to make a turn, slamming the reverse thrusters to slow down. That's when the cops caught up to him. It was simply too fast to fly around narrow passages at high speeds.

"We're getting nowhere," Cameron said from the safety of the backpack.

"I don't want to crash," Jimmy replied. He turned tightly, narrowly missing a cruiser that had appeared from behind an office building. "These cops are relentless. I'm trying not to cause an accident." If this were a game, he'd just force the police cars into traffic. But he behaved differently in the real world. Real people's lives were at stake.

"You'll never lose them in the mid-levels," Cameron said. "They have cameras on the corners of every building."

"What are you saying? We need to go up to the skyways? Every cop car will see us."

"Trust me. I'm an AI. I'm smarter than you."

Jimmy burst out laughing and then screamed, spinning the car sideways to avoid a protruding landing pad.

"Watch where you're going!"

"Then don't make jokes."

"I was being serious."

The police sirens screeched at them from behind, lights flashing in the rear-vision mirror. Another cruiser lined up alongside the Ason. Driver and passenger yelled at Jimmy to pull over.

"They're trying to box you in," Cameron said.

"I can see that! Why do AIs always feel the need to provide a commentary?"

"Get up to the skyway. Now!"

Jimmy whipped the car out of the police manoeuvre, careful not to trade paint, and angled the Ason up towards the nearest skyway. The hypercar lurched forwards, but the police stayed on his tail.

Jimmy noticed a red button on the steering wheel. "What does this button do?" Red buttons always did something awesome in movies.

Cameron connected to the Ason's computer while the car

approached the heavy traffic of the skyway. "The manual says it's a bass boost for the car's speaker system."

"That's all?"

"That's all."

Jimmy groaned as he joined the fast-moving traffic. Now he was even more nervous about scratching Chuck's car . . . Harlequin's car . . . the most expensive car he'd ever driven. Vehicles zoomed all around him on the six-lane, three-level arterial skyway.

"All right, Mr Smartypants, how do we lose the fuzz?"

"Give me a moment. I need to hack into the city's traffic management system."

"You can do that?"

An airbus merged lanes ahead of them, forcing Jimmy to dive under it, honking his horn as he passed. The Ason, despite being the most awesome car in the skyway, had a little squeak for a horn. Jimmy shrank in embarrassment.

"Of course I can," Cameron replied. "It runs on a network. It has firewalls, but I can break through."

Jimmy rose up to the middle layer of traffic. "Where were you hiding all this time? Imagine all the corporate secrets I could have uncovered if you worked with me at the newspaper."

Cameron didn't reply. Either he didn't like the idea, or he was busy committing cybercrimes. Either way, Jimmy left him to it. He needed to concentrate on the traffic. The police were still chasing him, though they were having a hard time getting through the stubborn traffic and had resorted to maintaining the chase from the skyway's edges. Jimmy couldn't see any way out of this. He'd failed, and it would be only a matter of time before either the police or Harlequin's goons caught his friends.

"Okay, I've just logged maintenance runs and detours along several major skyways," Cameron said. "Pretty soon, most northbound traffic will be diverted to this thorough-fare, and the skyway's boundary markers will expand to accommodate the increased load. I estimate a ten-lane, five-level transformation in about five minutes."

It didn't take quite so long. To Jimmy's left, a lower skyway was diverting upwards to join his. Floating traffic markers opened a wide on-ramp and extra lanes. Off to the right, in the distance, the same thing was happening.

Before too long, Jimmy was flying in the middle of the most congested skyway he'd ever experienced. Speed and flow remained constant, but it proved harder to merge and get to safe exit zones. Frustrated drivers blasted horns and shouted out of windows whenever someone got in the way. Jimmy found the button to close the roof, at least affording them some privacy and protection from angry drivers.

"The last thing we need is road rage," he said.

The police were all but lost in the commotion. With thousands of cars barrelling along, they had no hope.

"Now comes the tricky part," Cameron said. "We need to peel off from this route and descend to the hangar. It's down there."

Jimmy risked a glance out his window. "I see it. When I leave, I'll expose myself."

"You've done that plenty of times already," Cameron noted. "This time, speed is of the essence."

"No, I mean . . . oh, never mind. Doesn't this car have like a supersonic, bone-shattering, see-ya-later-suckers boost button?"

"Yes, I saw it in the manual. First, let's get out of the traffic."

Jimmy dropped and weaved the nimble car to the bottom left edge of the massive skyway and then peeled off, aiming for the spaceport. There were no police cars in sight.

"Okay, push the green button next to the gear stick."

He did so, and a panel opened up below the gear stick.

"Now, push the white button on the left."

Jimmy pushed that, and then his eyes went wide. Another panel opened within the first panel, and up came the most glorious of all red buttons he had ever seen. He silently prayed a thanks that it was red, true to all of his preconceptions.

"Push the red button."

Jimmy planted his whole palm on it and the Ason roared with otherworldly power. The force pushed him into his seat. Cameron, not strapped in and at that moment hovering in between the two seats, experienced the law of inertia. With the acceleration of the car, Cameron's hovering body went backwards, crashing through the Ason's rear window and out into the sky.

"Cameron!" Jimmy called. The Ason had already halved the distance to the hangar and there was no way he could turn back at this speed. Even the digital speedometer had maxed out at 999 kilometres per hour.

He figured he must look like a lunatic, soaring through the sky like some daredevil. As he neared the hangar, he saw a cluster of people standing outside. He recognised his friends. They waved at him, jumping and shouting. He overshot them at great speed, fought to raise the car, did a turning loop in the air, and slowed down enough to bring the vehicle safely into the hangar. The big double doors closed behind him.

The guys ran up to him, cheering.

"You did it!"

"You did it!"

"He did it!"

Jimmy jumped out, his legs like jelly. "I did it!"

"You did it!"

"I did it! I did it!"

They laughed victoriously, shook his hand, clapped him on the back. Then Chuck saw the hole in the back window.

"What happened here?" Chuck asked.

"Oh . . . that."

"And where's Cameron?"

"Uh, we hit the big red button, and Cameron went out the back window."

The hangar went silent.

"You lost Cameron?" Dave asked.

"No, no, he should be on his way. It happened nearby."

"Forget Cameron for now," Chuck said. "Look what happened to my car. Harlequin won't take this."

"Well . . . sure she will," Jimmy said. "It's just a window. I mean, at least I didn't scratch the paint."

Someone knocked on the hangar door, startling the group.

Chuck darted over to the door panel and looked through a peephole. He gasped. "She's here."

18

SWEET SUCCESS

Harlequin's black luxury sedan glided into the hangar, followed by a rigid container truck. The truck backed up to the Ason as Harlequin stepped out, arms open in surprise.

"I should put you guys on my crew," she said. "It took you less than six hours to deliver."

For a woman who had grown up around high-performance machines, Harlequin Grover just about drooled over Chuck's Ason 124X. It was one of only ten ever made, out of which it was one of only two made for human drivers. In a galaxy filled with intelligent lifeforms, that meant it was extremely rare.

"Why is the window broken?"

Jimmy ruffled his hair. "I had some robotic help, and it accidentally smashed through it when I engaged the boosters."

Harlequin stepped closer to Jimmy. "How did it feel?"

"The boosters? Like every inch of my body was being punched by evil leprechauns."

"Amazing, isn't it?" Harlequin said with a toothy grin. "I'll have to try it." She waved for her crew to load it into the truck.

"I wouldn't do it anywhere near this planet, if I were you," Chuck warned. "We had Shadow detectives casing my place, and the police chased Jimmy halfway here. This car is hot."

"Ohh, listen to you, Chuckie Boy," Harlequin said. "'Hot'. You sound like regular thief now."

Chuck stiffened. "This isn't my proudest moment. But if it saves my friends and screws over my ex-wife, then so be it."

"Yes, about that . . . " Harlequin gestured for the guys to follow her. They put distance between themselves and the Grover minions. "Now that you've shown that you're well and truly a part of this arrangement, we can go ahead with the rest of your plan. My crews are already on their way to your other houses. They'll take your cars and bring them to me. Even if your wife has already acquired some, we're willing to track them down and take them for ourselves. You'll sort out the insurance problems and any police investigations? Keep them off our scent?"

"Of course," Chuck said. His original plan had been to destroy the cars, but giving them to Harlequin to buy back his friend's lives was a more noble action.

"Good. Oh, it's so much easier to steal cars when the owner lets us do it."

"I'm glad I could help. Actually, now that I think about it, I have a space yacht, too. If you can take that, you'll be my best friend."

"Hey!" Dave said.

Chuck silenced him with a wave. "What do you say?"

Harlequin scratched her chin. "A space yacht is a bit harder to hide. I'll see what I can do. It's not like you're going to use it ever again, right?"

Chuck nodded.

"Well, boys, this has been great day. Now let's never speak again, and don't you even think about telling the police about our arrangement."

"Wouldn't dream of it, Harley," Eddie said.

"I told you not to call me that."

"You'll always be little Harley to me."

"Ms Grover is probably more suitable," Jimmy said.

Dave preferred "Doughnut Thief", but the sudden change in Harlequin's expression sealed his mouth shut.

"I say we part ways now," Harlequin said. Just like that, the excited girl in her had transformed back to the steely crime boss. Her eyes went cold, her mouth unsmiling. "Safe travels, gentlemen."

With that, the guys shuffled up *Liberty*'s ramp and crammed into the elevator. No one spoke. Even Eve gave them time to process.

"Well, that was unsettling," Dave finally said.

"Everything about the Grover Clan is unsettling," Eddie said.

Chuck grunted. "Except when half of Compton sued them. They were *settling* then."

They laughed at Chuck's legal pun.

"I say we get out of here as soon as possible," Dave said.

Everyone else agreed. The elevator doors slid open and they all went to the cockpit. While Chuck and Jimmy were out committing crimes (to which they would henceforth never admit), Eddie had been re-downloading and re-installing a full star chart suite. They now had a full galaxy open to them, except for the Outer Crux–Scutum Arm. No one liked going there. It was the Bermuda Triangle of the galaxy. Too many anomalies for comfort.

Harlequin and her lackeys were leaving the hangar as the guys settled into the cockpit. They were glad to be rid of her, and they shared her sentiments about never crossing paths again just as Cameron zoomed into the open hangar.

"Hey, good thing we didn't leave without him," Jimmy said with a nervous laugh. "I'm sure he's all right."

Eddie opened the entryway for Cameron and the little drone zipped inside. Then he let Eve pilot the ship outside.

"I'm glad you give me this responsibility, Eddie," Eve said. "No more damaging hangars."

"You'll never let me live that down, will you?"

"Nope."

Eve took *Liberty* out with precision, cleared the codes with flight control, and then roared upwards. Cameron joined them a moment later.

"Welcome back," Jimmy said.

"Sure, no thanks to you," Cameron quipped. "The force of my expulsion shut me down. I dropped a full five hundred metres before rebooting. But don't worry, it *was* my fault. I should have secured myself."

"Let's leave it behind us, like we're all doing to this planet."

"Agreed." Cameron hovered over near Dave so he could inspect the drone.

"You know, Cam," Jimmy said, "you're all right. You guys should see how he performed out there. Like a pro."

"You weren't recording anything, were you?" Chuck asked.

"Of course I was," Cameron replied, spinning to face Chuck. "I film everything."

"Delete it."

Cameron turned to Dave, who nodded. "Master approves the order," Cameron said. He whirred and buzzed. "Footage deleted."

Liberty shook gently as it passed through the upper atmosphere. Then everything darkened as they were once more back in space. Eclat hung off the port bow, still aglow with the lights of gambling, debauchery, and crime. It felt like ages since they'd docked there.

They guys sat in silence, enjoying the peace of space with its distinct lack of police sirens and thugs threatening to kill them. They watched an endless stream of freighters and passenger liners gliding in and out of the system. Finally, when *Liberty* reached its calculated jump point, Dave made the announcement.

"Time to go to Paradise," he said.

The ship jolted into FTL drive and the stars went psychedelic. *Liberty* was crossing her way to what the advertisements called "the most beautiful spot in the galaxy".

"Who wants a beer?" Eddie asked.

They went to the lounge room and Jimmy marched right up to the pinball machine—they were still trying to get a human in first place. Chuck and Dave plonked themselves on the couch, and Eddie rounded the bar to the fridge. He handed them their drinks and then raised his bottle.

"To Paradise!" they echoed, and drank quietly.

"You want to know what I'm looking forward to on this garden world?" Dave asked. The others gestured for him to continue. He counted off the list on his hand. "Nobody threatening to kill us, good weather, good food, no wooden cages, and real toilets."

They laughed. In a little over twelve hours, they would get just that.

19

THE COSMIC BUBBLE BURSTS AGAIN

Eve announced *Liberty*'s imminent arrival at Paradise in her usual soft voice. Her gentle tone woke Jimmy up from his nap, made Dave quickly finish his business on the toilet, broke Eddie's concentration and forced him to lose a game of pinball, and motivated Chuck to run to his room to comb his hair. They all convened in the cockpit just as *Liberty*'s FTL drive disengaged.

"The first thing I'm going to do is get a coffee," Chuck announced. But as the ship drew closer to Paradise, his excited face fell flat.

What they saw devastated them. Advertised as a tourist getaway, the planet and its massive orbital space station looked nothing of the sort. In fact, it was well and truly dead. If a sloth had chewed off three of your fingers, you could still count all visible ships with the rest of your fingers with plenty of time to faint due to blood loss.

"Um, I guess we should check in at the space station?" Eddie said.

He took direct control of *Liberty* and piloted her towards the huge circular station. The others watched in confusion at the

144

eeriness of the situation. Eddie signalled the huge construct before them. He wanted to know what hangar to land in.

"Are you serious, mate?" Dave asked. "Just pick one. They're all empty."

They approached, but on closer inspection they found it to be quite rundown. One of the ships they'd thought was moored was actually half embedded into the station's hull, twisted metal rippling out from the point of impact.

"The place looks deserted," Chuck said.

"What do you reckon?" Eddie asked. "Should we go to the space station or straight to the planet?"

"I think we should try the station first," Chuck said. His brow was furrowed and his eyes squinted as he surveyed the quietude outside. "Let's do things properly."

Eddie went to the nearest hangar door and it opened automatically. The interior was still and dark. He hesitated before piloting *Liberty* inside. The doors closed behind them, sealing them in.

"Eve, what's the atmosphere like in this hangar?" Eddie asked.

"Deadly, Eddie. Truly deadly. You will die if you go out there. I mean, you will be properly dead."

"Thanks for explaining that to me."

"I figured since you guys have cheated death several times since I've known you, your luck may run out soon. So I'm looking out for you."

"She's good value," Jimmy said with a nod.

"Well, I don't feel like suiting up to walk out there," Eddie told them. "It's not what I like to do when I get to a holiday spot." He tried to hail someone . . . anyone.

They stayed there for five minutes, sending message after message, hoping that there was someone on the station to answer them. Finally, rather abruptly, they got a garbled audio response with a link to a video source. Eddie put it up on the vidscreen and they all jumped at the sight of the alien who looked back at them. A face peered out amid rolls of brown flesh.

Jimmy leaned close to Dave. "The last time I saw something like that," he whispered, "I flushed it."

"Hi," Eddie began. "Uh, we're here to visit Paradise." He paused, not knowing what else to say. The alien looked dumbfounded, moving its hands around on something in front of it off-screen. "Uh, can we go to the planet?"

"Then again," Jimmy continued, almost to himself now, "it's so ugly it could scare the crap *out* of a toilet."

Dave hit him. "Mind your manners."

The alien started yammering something in its language. Then its voice changed to English as it fiddled with a dial on its sleeve. " . . . glad I figured out how to work this stupid thing. I've been here for so long and it's been ages since anyone has come here. Nobody bothers to contact me from the planet anymore. I was going crazy talking to myself all the time. You know just yesterday I actually had an argument with myself, and I lost! Oh, I know times have been rough on the planet, too, but if they could just send a ship, just one ship, or a little shuttle—anything to come get me. But no, nothing. They just left me here. Wasn't my fault I was stuck in a utility tunnel when they did the evacuations. Now they won't waste anyone's time or money to come get me. You probably saw the crashed ship when you came in. That was my attempt to remotely pilot one of the few remaining vessels moored to the exterior dock. But, hey, guess what? I'm only a lowly maintenance technician. I know zilch about flying a half-billion EsCe luxury yacht. Now it's wrecked. Not that the owner would be coming back for it. If he was, he'd have been here by now—"

"Hey, shut up for a minute," Chuck said. He could feel the throb of a headache starting. The alien stopped and looked at him like Chuck had committed a cardinal sin. "What's going on here?"

The alien looked side-to-side, its oily, rubbery cheeks and neck rolling grotesquely with the movement. "Tragedy, that's what. But I won't tell you any more unless you take me down to the planet. I've been stuck here for goodness knows how long."

Everyone looked at Eddie. His ship, his choice.

"He looks trustworthy," Eve said.

"What air do you breathe?" Eddie asked him.

"Pure hydrogen sulphide. Once I realised no one was coming for me, I converted the whole space station's air supply to hydrogen sulphide. Oh, don't exit your ship! I should have told you that first. My bad."

"Death, Eddie," Eve said in the background. "Death."

"Do you have a breathing apparatus or enviro suit?" Eddie asked him.

"Yes."

"Okay, come to our ship."

"Where are you?"

"How should I know? It's your spaceport. You find us."

"Yeah. Right. See you soon."

It took the little guy an hour to find them. But when he emerged in the hangar, they saw he was not quite as little as the vidscreen made out. He was enormous in height and width, and his enviro suit made him look even bigger. He carried with him four huge bags, probably with his personal effects.

"Subject approaching ship," Eve announced. "Entering pressure and decontamination chamber. Cleansing of horrible odours the likes of which you would never want to smell. Still cleansing. Cleansed. Subject is entering elevator—"

Eddie squeezed the bridge of his nose as he listened to Eve's painful commentary of the visitor's movements. But she insisted on keeping an eye on him. Something didn't add up, she said.

"The elevator has reached max speed," Eve continued. "Rising, higher, higher. Elevator at current deck level. Doors opening, this time to full width so as not to delay our wide guest."

The guys left the cockpit to meet the alien technician.

Chuck, the tallest of the four, found it uncomfortable to look up at the newcomer's face, not just because he was unpleasant to look at, but for the sheer height of him. The alien's helmeted head barely cleared the ceiling.

"Hello," the alien said. "Your elevator is painfully slow." His mouth moved in his own language, but a helmet speaker projected an English translation. "Thank you so much for letting me come with you. It's such a short trip to the planet, you know, but no one has wanted to come for me. They even stopped answering my calls. I hope they haven't all died. That would be horrible. I'd be all alone on the planet. You'd stay with me, won't you?" He stared at his hosts.

"No," was all Jimmy said.

"That's Jimmy," Eddie said. "This is Dave and Chuck. I'm Eddie. Cameron's over there, and this is Eve." He lifted his hands up like the Pope.

"Hello," Eve said cheerfully.

"Oh, are you David Winkle?" the alien asked.

Dave tensed. How could this random being possibly know who he was? "Yes."

The alien reached into one of the bags and pulled out a package. It was a narrow rectangular box about thirty centimetres long. "I've been waiting for you. Got something I'm supposed to deliver to you, and *only* to you. A courier left it here at the station, but he wouldn't take me with him. Said I was now the one to give this to you." He gave the package to Dave.

Dave tore open the wrapping paper. "Hey, my Weight-Master 3000!"

"You also owe me 40 EsCes, because you were charged an out-of-system delivery fee."

"Oh, okay." Dave reached into his pocket for his phone.

"Nah, just kidding!" he said. He laughed while the English translation still spoke. "You actually did get charged. I paid, but you don't owe me anything. Consider it my way of paying my fare planetside."

"That's awfully kind of you."

"What is your name?" Eddie asked.

"My name is Elsrabbledomkapfromarpur."

The guys digested it like stale bread. Eddie nodded. "Right, we'll call you 'El' for short. Let's head off. You can tell us what happened here while we travel."

♥♣♦♠

E<small>L RELATED THE STRANGE</small> event that had befallen Paradise. It seemed, in a nutshell, that Paradise became so paradisiacal for its human holidaymakers that it decided to "destroy itself". The planet quite literally rebelled against the tourist industry that had so disrespectfully built itself on top of many square kilometres of natural beauty.

The guys didn't fully understand this until Eddie pierced the planet's atmosphere and brought *Liberty* closer to the green surface. A well-designed network of streets, hotels, shops, entertainment centres, and infrastructure was overrun with vegetation.

"An ecological apocalypse," Jimmy said. "Only instead of people destroying nature, nature destroyed us." He whipped out his digipad and started writing.

"What are you doing?" Chuck asked him.

"I'm going to write an article on this and publish it," he told him. "Now that I don't have a job, I'll probably do freelance work. The galaxy needs to know what happened here, because we obviously didn't."

"Oh, they sent distress calls and the news media did report on it," El said. "But you know what the media is like. So much happens in this galaxy, it's hard to find the time to report on everything for any reasonable length of time. Wouldn't surprise me if all it got was a single line in a newspaper: 'Plants destroy resort town'."

Eddie flew *Liberty* above the green, empty tourist city, obeying El's directions. Even El was surprised at what Paradise Central looked like.

"I saw it happening over vidscreen," El told them. He stood in the cockpit—no seat was large enough for him. "All the plants attacked overnight. Tree roots brought down multi-storey buildings and grass forced itself through roads and footpaths. Vines took over whole city blocks, grabbing hold of buildings through windows and doors, choking the structures to death. Trees committed suicide, toppling on anything and anyone beneath them. It was total and complete chaos."

Dave, for one, held conflicted feelings about the situation. On the one hand, he felt depressed at having gone through so much to get here, only to have his reward dashed before him. But on the other hand, he was happy the planet had fought back against people who didn't care what they were doing to it. The planet had reclaimed its own sovereignty.

"So, does this mean there are no working coffee machines down there?" You know who asked this.

"I don't suppose there are," El said. "Not that I care. Coffee is nasty stuff—gives me the runs. Let's land now. See that square over there? There should be plenty of room."

"Is it safe?" Eddie wondered aloud.

"I don't know."

Eddie dropped the ship and landed on a section of the public square where the vegetation was sparse. Eve told them that the air outside was a little high in oxygen but that they would be safe without enviro suits. El went out first, since he pretty much filled the elevator by himself. When the guys made it out ten minutes later, they found El staring at the ruins of a once flourishing city. The air tasted clean and fresh. Cameron filmed everything.

Dave took a deep breath, savouring the peace and quiet, closing his eyes to the destruction around him. Oh, if ever he was to go blind, this would be the place to do it. Then the screeching voice of Jennifer Moseby filled his mind and he frowned, opening his eyes again to find his friends a few paces away. He rushed to join them.

El took his human guests through what used to be the shopping district, showing them the damage and seeing first-hand what the planet had done. He said he had never imagined it to be so destructive. The video footage just hadn't done it justice. There were many buildings reduced to rubble, greenery shooting out of cracks like little victory flags. Vehicles of all sorts were turned over and crushed. Jimmy continued to write down all these details, while Cameron recorded for him.

Dave pointed out a lone figure in the distance and grew excited at the prospect of meeting a survivor. Upon drawing closer, however, they realised it was a robot, still performing its task of walking back and forth across an intersection on the main boulevard through the shopping district. El said those robots used to escort elderly holidaymakers across the road. There was not a single person in sight. Not even the remains of any who might have died.

The breeze rustled leaves and the calls and noises of different animals and insects sounded like some far-off orchestra. Despite the obvious scenes of destruction and ruin, however, the place was serene. Eddie liked it. He felt at peace. Chuck would have, too, were it not for the nagging demands of a short black.

They about-faced to return to the ship, but Chuck stayed back. When they realised he wasn't with them, they stopped and watched him. He had his back to them. He knelt down and brushed blades of grass with his palm. Then he tipped onto his backside and sat on the broken road, face in his hands. His friends rushed over to him.

"Mate, you all right?" Dave asked. He crouched next to the lawyer.

Jimmy put away his digipad. "What's happening?"

Chuck pulled his hands away from his face. His cheeks were wet, his eyes red with sadness and despair. He turned his face away from them, sniffled and took a breath. "This was supposed to be our little getaway," he said softly, his voice shaking.

"It still is, mate," Dave said. "We've had a ball, haven't we, guys?"

"Yeah," Eddie said. "Yeah, think of what we've done since leaving Earth."

"It doesn't matter that this place is a dump," Jimmy told him. "We'll find another paradise."

"No," Chuck told them and faced them. His voice carried the usual firmness they were familiar with. But then his lips quivered again, and right then he looked like a broken man. "Paradise was supposed to be the end of the line for me. What with the divorce and everything, my life's gone belly-up. I wanted to bring you guys here so we could enjoy ourselves one last time . . . for old time's sake."

Jimmy straightened. His mouth opened, closed, and then opened again. "You were going to kill yourself here?"

Chuck arched his eyebrows. "No, nothing that drastic." He paused, and for a moment they thought he might have been lying. "I have a house here. I wanted to spend time here with my friends and then stay by myself when it was time for you three to go. But now it looks like I dragged you through muddy waters for nothing. This place has nothing for us. I have nothing anymore." He hung his head low.

"You still have us, Chucky," Jimmy said quietly.

A smile crept into the corner of Chuck's mouth. "Yeah, I do. You're the only ones who care about me. Betty hates my guts. My daughters don't talk to me. The partners at my firm only care if I make money or if I'm coming back to hold the reins. All I have left are you three."

"Now that's luck if I ever did see it," Jimmy said.

"And I'm not even Irish." Chuck sniffed a laugh. "I'm sorry I dragged you here, guys." They all rejected the apology as unnecessary, but he insisted. "No, really, there's nothing for us here."

"You said you had a house," Dave said. "Why don't we go visit it?"

"It's probably destroyed," Chuck told him.

"Do you really think that would stop us?" Eddie asked.

Chuck grinned. "No. We're the most stubborn bastards I know. All right, let's go. Maybe the coffee machine still works."

They helped him up and motioned El to join them. He'd stepped away to give them some privacy. Chuck rubbed his eyes and had a good look again at his surroundings, pausing at some movement nearby.

"What's that?" he asked, pointing. "You see it?"

They stared.

Eddie stepped in front of them. "Well, I'll be damned . . . "

"It's a human," El said.

They stood in silence as the human slowly approached. But the nearer this fellow being came, the more the guys realised something was wrong . . . or different. The human was female—nothing wrong or different about that. But she wore tattered clothes, stained green and brown as if she'd been crawling through earth and vegetation. Her skin was deep green, and she had little pink and white flowers in her hair.

She stopped a few metres from them. "Who are *you*?" she asked, her voice as cool as a refreshing breeze on a hot day.

Eddie introduced everyone. "We have travelled a long way to get here. El comes from the space station. Who are you?"

"They called me Sequoia, but my birth name is Ichika."

Jimmy busied himself on his digipad while Cameron filmed the whole exchange.

Chuck cleared his throat. "Forgive me for being forward, but may I ask: *what* are you?"

She faced Chuck. "You are the one who was crying. Why?"

Chuck swallowed hard and straightened himself. He wondered whether he should explain himself to this stranger—this *strange* stranger—but then figured he had nothing else to lose. "I am a man who has gained everything in life and then seen nearly all of it taken from him by a woman he dearly loved. I have lost my family, the respect of my work colleagues, and most of the fruits of my labour. I had a house here. It was my last refuge, somewhere I could go to do some soul searching before returning to the big, bad galaxy. But there's nothing left." He looked around. "It's all gone."

She walked up to Chuck, slowly, deliberately, until she was less than an arm's length away. She tentatively raised her hand to his face. When he didn't resist, she let her hand rest on his cheek. She smelled of petrichor—the pleasant odour of raindrops and wet earth. She caressed his cheek. Her hand was surprisingly warm. It had been a long time since Chuck experienced this sort of affection.

"Show me where you live," she said. "I want to see the damage."

Chuck stared into her eyes. They were sad, maybe empathetic, and yet they somehow held a glimmer of . . . what was it? Hope?

"You still haven't told us what you are," Dave said softly.

Her hand returned to her waist and she blinked at Dave. "Take me to this man's home, and I will explain everything."

20

THE TREE HOUSE

The coffee machine didn't work. In fact, it was so busted up, it no longer resembled a coffee machine at all. A tough green vine had wiggled its way into every nook and cranny of the Chinese-made, Italian-stamped contraption, busting the thing open and clogging it in every spot imaginable. A mess of plastic parts and brown beans littered the kitchen bench and floor. Chuck gave the scene one look and shuffled out of the destroyed room.

Even from a distance the house looked overrun. Half of it had crumbled away under what would have been a terrible vegetative onslaught, while the rest of it was now so intertwined with the vine that the two were just about inseparable. The place stank of earth and rotting plants, and some rude animal had seen fit to claim the master bedroom as a defecation chamber. The clean-freak lawyer turned his nose up to that and promptly closed the bedroom door, ushering his friends away, but not before Cameron took a good, long recording of the mess.

Chuck had built his house on a hill away from the holiday resort. It overlooked the rolling green fields below and the beach beyond. They stood in what used to be his lounge room, staring at the scene through the curved, panoramic window that ran the full length of the room. The glass had shattered where a vine had busted through, leaving sharp, jagged edges and a spray of little sparkling pieces all over the hardwood floor.

Jimmy sat on a vine stem, dangling his legs with careless regard. "This place is trashed."

Chuck stood with his hands in his pockets, still looking at the beach in the distance, apparently oblivious to Jimmy's statement of the obvious. He turned to Sequoia. "All right. You've seen my house. Now tell me who and what you are, and why you wanted to come here."

Sequoia brushed past a dangling plant. It rustled and stuck to her as if connected by a magnet. Then it disengaged, hung upright, shimmered animatedly and dropped back to its original position.

"My birth name is Ichika Sato," she began, "though nobody calls me that anymore. I was an overworked and underpaid HR manager. I came to Paradise to recharge, much like you. But while I slept, the planet rebelled. *We* rebelled."

"What do you mean by 'we'," Dave said. "Did the tourists and locals have a part in it?"

"No," Sequoia replied. "Not at all. It was entirely the planet's doing. The planet is an intelligent life form, just like any civilised being who visited or worked here. It lives and breathes, it builds and grows, it plans and accomplishes. The only problem it had was that it could not communicate in any way that you would understand . . . until now."

Chuck looked out the broken window at the expanse of untouched greenery. Sure, forests were alive in that they were self-contained ecosystems. But intelligent? Could a forest think?

"Why is everything different now?" Chuck asked her.

"Because the planet now has people who can speak for it."

Sequoia stepped into the middle of the room, spread her arms out and closed her eyes. The vines rocked, the leaves rustled, flower stems danced.

"Whoa," Dave exclaimed. "What's happening?"

Jimmy stopped writing and just stared at the phenomenon. Eddie, usually the one to inspect anything, stayed resolutely still. A moment later, Sequoia opened her eyes, smiled, lowered her arms, and the vegetation ceased its movement.

"I am the planet, and the planet is me," she said. "We have achieved mutual symbiosis—a biological transformation. We are hybrids of every race that was here when the Green Rebellion happened."

"'We'?" Eddie asked.

"There are many of us. Some visitors escaped, but many were trapped on the surface. Unfortunately, some died in the destruction of Paradise Central." She dropped her head at that. "But for those who survived, the planet offered us a new life. Some rejected it, but most accepted. We are now walking, talking hybrids, emissaries of the world, forever changed and yet forever unchanging."

The guys stood breathless before her. If what she said was right, then a new "alien" race had just been born. Dave, so totally bewildered by the experience, pinched himself and sat down, his head spinning. Jimmy went back to note-taking.

Chuck and Eddie were full of questions, and they fought to be the first to ask them. But it was Jimmy's loud voice that Sequoia heard over them.

"But how do you . . . where do you . . . ?" Jimmy fumbled.

"Our waste is now carbon dioxide and oxygen, if that is what you were asking," Sequoia said.

"Really?" Eddie asked, turning to Jimmy. "*That* was your question?"

Jimmy shrugged and returned to his digipad. "Won't know until I find out."

Chuck took his chance while Eddie was distracted. "Tell us, why did Paradise need or want emissaries? What does it want to say?"

"Now that's a question!" Eddie said.

"Your answer is twofold," Sequoia said. "It took immense energy to launch the Green Rebellion. Despite its success, Paradise now needs help to repair the damage done to root systems and natural habitats. Land in several locations has been ruined. The planet needs us to undo the damage it did to itself when it fought back. In this way, we are more than emissaries. We are gardeners, landscapers, builders. Our second purpose was to secure the long-term future of this planet. Eventually, people will return and may rebuild what we have destroyed. Worse, they may exploit the planet's natural resources. Those resources are not free to take, nor will Paradise stand for more destruction. We understand that we cannot stop civilisation from returning to this corner of the galaxy. In light of that, we need trustees who understand the sentience of Paradise, and who will work with us to ensure any future civilised activity is sustainable and environmentally friendly. The planet must be protected from further harm. We cannot have a repeat of the exploitation that occurred here before."

Chuck went into Full Lawyer Mode. He clasped his hands behind his back and paced the room in deep thought. Everyone gave him the quiet he needed to think. Finally, from the other end of the room, Chuck faced everyone.

"I have no ideas," he announced.

"We could rebuild the resort," Eddie said.

"What good would that do?" Chuck asked. "It's like making the same mistake all over again."

"No," Eddie said, getting all excited. "Not if we do it right. We need to 'touch the land lightly'. It's an architectural phrase. We build, but we respect the land we're building on, the resources we gather, the . . . the methods we use for construction. Let's build the galaxy's first one hundred per cent eco-friendly resort city."

"Yeah," Jimmy said. "And we should teach all our visitors about what happened here. They should learn about Paradise and the emissaries. Sequoia said Paradise wants trustees."

"Who? Us?" Chuck asked.

Sequoia sighed deeply and the vines rumbled. "I must confer with the planet."

She sat on a vine and closed her eyes. Everyone moved to where Chuck stood to give her some room. The forest outside started swaying, leaves dancing on their twigs, tree limbs creaking and groaning. Birds, startled by the movement, squawked and fluttered into the sky away from the moving forest canopy. It was strange seeing trees move as if subject to gusty winds, and yet no wind came through the broken windows. Sequoia's audience with the planet must have sparked a deep discussion.

And then, as if a storm had passed, the trees went still. Sequoia opened her eyes and beckoned everyone to come to her.

"Paradise wants you as her trustee," she said, pointing to Chuck.

"What?" he asked. "But I don't know the first thing about building a resort."

"You don't have to," Eddie said, landing a hand on his shoulder, "we'll help you. And you're a lawyer—I'm sure you can organise a building project."

"The emissaries are at your disposal," Sequoia said.

"Wait, wait," Chuck said. He held up his hands and pulled away from the group. "We can't just move in and start building. People owned this resort. There are investors."

Dave grinned from the back.

"What's that face for?" Chuck asked.

"You're right," Dave said. "There are investors—investors of a *destroyed* resort city. How cheap do you reckon those shares are?"

Chuck shrugged.

Dave showed everyone his phone. "One point three EsCes per share, down from ninety-eight point six EsCes pre-Rebellion. There are fifteen million shares in Paradise Inc. We could buy this place and the company outright."

Chuck took the phone and inspected the numbers. "He's right!"

"It seems everything is in your favour," Sequoia said.

"There's still a lot of work to do, but we can do it," Chuck told her. He looked at his friends. "Do we all agree to become part owners of Paradise Inc? Are we all able to rebuild an entire city and associated resort?"

"Hell yeah!" Jimmy said. "I don't have a job to go back to. I could be the marketing and tourism manager."

"And I don't want to work at Sremmacs anymore," Dave said quietly. "I'll handle all the accounts and financials for this place."

"Eddie?" Chuck asked. "What do you say? You're the only one who still has a wife and kids."

Eddie nodded. "I built *Liberty* to escape Earth. It's getting too crowded, too polluted. Look at that ocean." He pointed out at the pristine waters beyond the forest. The crystal-clear sea met a wide, snaking line of bright yellow sand before the greenery started. "I'd love to do it, but I need to talk to Christie and the kids first."

"There is one small problem, though," Dave said. "What do we know about running a city? Or rejuvenating a planet?"

"Don't worry," Jimmy said. "Politicians don't know how to run cities, either. But a handful of them do a half-decent job of it."

Eddie put a hand on Dave's shoulder. "Half the fun of running a business is learning how to do it and not screwing up too much along the way."

"And you will have the support of the emissaries," Sequoia added.

Chuck smiled. "I'm glad you've all said yes. It will be hard work, but I know it'll be easier if we do it together. And besides, from what I've seen, we could all use a fresh start." He faced Eddie. "How sure are you that Christie will say 'yes'?"

"She hates our neighbours, so I'm pretty sure."

Chuck nodded and turned to Sequoia. "We'll do it."

"Paradise thanks you," Sequoia said. Every plant in sight rustled as if shouting in excitement. Chuck extended a hand, shook Sequoia's, sealing the deal.

"We have a lot of work to do," he said.

Jimmy stepped forward, pointing a thumb at his chest. "I know how to paint."

"I have my screwspanhamulesawilevelplifench," Eddie told them.

"I don't know how to build," Dave said. "But I have muscles."

"Yeah, okay," Chuck said, stifling a laugh. "I didn't mean that kind of work. We'll be the project managers. I mean, we need to contact my stockbroker, get the wheels in motion. Then I'll have to find an architect, a town planner, a civil engineer . . . so many people to contact. And they'll all need to appreciate building in tandem with the environment . . . " He walked away, almost talking to himself.

Eddie faced El. The alien, who had been standing aside the whole time, made a gurgling noise and they all turned to him. He swung his little arms back and forth. He tried to clasp them behind his back, but his body was too round and his arms too short to reach, so he opted just to leave them hanging at his side.

"Will you join us, El?" Eddie asked.

"I think it is nice that you want to rebuild," El said, "though I do hope that you and the plants can maintain friendly relations. You seem like nice people, so I have high hopes for you. Me, I would like to go home."

"To the space station?" Jimmy asked.

"No, not the space station. I mean my homeworld. I've lived here long enough, and I want to return to my family."

Eddie nodded and queried the others for their input.

"Uh, yeah, okay," Chuck said. "I don't see why not. We have some stuff to do before we begin here. And we are your only ticket out of here anyway."

"Lovely," El said. He waved his little arms about excitedly. "Thank you so much! It's not far to go. My homeworld is in the next star system."

"Well," Chuck said, "like I mentioned, we have a lot to do, so we should get moving. On our way to El's homeworld, I can start writing a business plan for the rebuild."

They shuffled out of Chuck's destroyed house, careful to avoid the vegetation and thick vines now that they knew of the planet's sentience. When they stepped outside into the fresh afternoon air, they found hundreds of emissaries waiting for them. These people were once citizens of the galaxy—tourists, local workers, mothers and fathers, children. Now they were an extension of the planet. All faced their new trustees and clapped. It sounded, fittingly, like raindrops.

"The emissaries are excited about the next stage in Paradise's life," Sequoia noted. "May we not repeat what happened before."

"We'll do our best," Chuck said. Nothing was pollution-free. Even *Liberty* landing and taking off polluted the air somewhat.

The emissaries, still clapping, cleared a path so the guys could get to *Liberty*, where she sat gleaming in the sun, a hull of metal juxtaposed against the natural beauty of the rolling, forested hills behind her.

"By the way," Sequoia said as they stopped at *Liberty*'s ramp, "I like your ship. It looks like a watermelon."

Eddie bit his tongue, then realised it was probably a compliment from this half-human, half-plant being.

They shook hands and bid farewell, promising to return as soon as possible. Dave felt a little sad when the entry door closed. It cut off the applause completely, and shut away the beautifully fresh scent of clean air and fragrant flowers that wafted around outside. He wished he could bottle it up and take it with him.

Chuck insisted on squeezing into the elevator with El. He had no time to waste, and he was willing to endure the discomfort of being squashed against the elevator wall on the slow ride up.

"I do apologise for my size," El said.

"No, don't mention it," Chuck said. He tried to laugh to lighten the mood, but he couldn't breathe enough to do that. "It takes all sizes to fill the galaxy."

"Too right, too right," El said.

The elevator opened. But El didn't move.

"You waiting for something?" Chuck asked.

"Oh, sorry, I thought you would go first. You said you were busy."

They bundled out and the elevator went back down to the others.

"I'm sorry to leave you, but there's much to be done. Feel free to relax in the lounge room. We have a pinball machine."

When Eddie made it to the upper deck, he found El playing pinball with one hand because his arms were too short to reach both flipper buttons at once.

"On my way to the leader board!" El exclaimed.

"Oh . . . great," Eddie said. If he had two aliens on the leader board, then he would have to work twice as hard to knock them off. And if El managed to overtake Shibb in first place, then he'd be working ten times harder. The guys had a running bet on who could take first place—the winner wouldn't have to do any cleaning on *Liberty* for an entire year.

"Hey guys, come in here. El thinks he can beat us at pinball."

"It's on, big fella," Jimmy said, appearing out of nowhere. Eddie could have sworn he'd gone to his cabin.

"Eve, take us to the next closest star system, please," Eddie said. "We've got some pinball to play."

21

A GOOD DEED IS DONE

THE SHORT TRIP TO El's planet was anything but boring. While he flogged them at pinball, El regaled them with stories about Paradise Central and funny work tales, and reminisced about his home. He had the guys in stitches with his antics. Dave, for one, couldn't remember the last time his cheeks hurt so much from laughing so hard.

They approached El's homeworld. It was a brown ball with swirling white clouds and deep green seas. Eve said the atmosphere would kill them in an instant if they didn't wear enviro suits, and El nodded.

"Where do we land?" Eddie asked. "I don't see a space station or port."

"Oh, just land anywhere," El told them. "We don't bother about that." He directed Eddie to his clan-city, squirming with excitement at being home after many years away.

"Seems like a nice place," Dave said.

"It is, it is," El said. "I grew up here. We used to go exploring in the nearby caves as youngsters. Once, we came across a rathmar nest and ran for our lives. The adults collapsed that cave later that night."

"What's a rathmar?" Jimmy asked. "Sounds like something I could write about."

"They're ferocious beasts that feed on flesh and hunt in packs. They prefer the coolness of the caves for hatching their young."

"Beasts, eh?" Chuck began. "How big are they?"

El looked around the cockpit, sizing up the room, and Chuck raised his eyebrows in wonderment. Then El spotted a pen by the astrogation table and held it up for the guys to see. "About the length of this."

"I see," Chuck said. His mouth twitched as he tried to hold in a laugh. "Quite scary."

"Very scary, very dangerous," El said. He left the cockpit.

Eddie found a large plain on which to land, setting *Liberty* down near some other dust-covered vessels. Wind gusts threw heavy particles against *Liberty*'s viewports, almost sounding like grains of salt in a shaker.

"You know we'll have to clean the ship someday," Eve said.

"Yeah," Eddie said. "It's a shame you can't clean yourself."

"Believe me, I wish I could. You lot have no idea how to keep this ship clean and tidy."

"We do our best, Eve," Eddie told her, and then stood and left the cockpit. El had gathered his belongings and was quietly chatting to the others by the elevator.

"Won't you come with me?" El asked. "I'll show you around."

"We should get going, El," Chuck told him. "We have some errands to run. The sooner we do them, the safer Paradise will be."

"We'll visit you when we can," Eddie said.

"I look forward to it," El said. "I may even go back to Paradise to see you, too."

Dave smiled. "You'd be more than welcome."

"Well, if you need any help, you know where to find me."

They guys nodded and thanked him for his support.

"I will say," El continued, "that I find this a kind gesture you've done for me. I've dreamed of returning home for so long. I thought I was going to die on that space station. But then you four appeared and saved me."

Eddie chuckled. "Really, it was pure luck."

"No, seriously, I am very grateful. And just from the short time we've been together, I've seen you for what you truly are. You are good people, kind, generous, and I do hope your plans for Paradise succeed. I know you'll look after the place." He smiled in his own strange way, lips curling out, bearing dark green teeth. Then he looked down. "Now, these bags—"

"Yes," Chuck said, "let's help you with those."

El stopped him with a gloved hand. "No. They're for you. When I accepted that no one was coming back to get me, I pillaged the whole spaceport. You'll find all sorts of valuables and goodies in those bags. They're yours to keep. It's my way of saying thank you."

The guys didn't know what to say. They refused at first, but El insisted. They managed some words of appreciation, but everyone was too embarrassed to consider the topic further. Big El, grotesque and lonely, had a heart of gold.

El smiled. "Safe travels. Wherever you go, don't ever forget the kindness you showed to this stranger. I never will." With that he turned his ponderous body and stepped into the elevator, waving goodbye as the doors closed.

"What a nice guy," Jimmy said. The elevator's motors whirred. Jimmy bent down and opened one of the bags. "Whoa! It's filled with jewellery!"

"Oh, no, that's people's stuff," Dave said. "I don't feel right taking that."

"And this—" Jimmy started as he opened another bag. "Is this foreign currency?" He lifted a handful of hard cash. "There's still cash in the galaxy?"

"Looks like it," Chuck told him. "And according to galactic law, what's in those bags belongs to us. Scavenger's rights."

"We can put it towards the resort," Eddie said.

Dave folded his arms and acquiesced. "I guess so. But we'll need a lot more than that."

"I know," Chuck told him, "and we'll get it, too, don't you worry. Once I sell off some of my own holdings and we pool resources, we can make a takeover bid."

"You're the man, Chuck," Eddie said. He nudged Jimmy with his foot, jolting the journalist's attention away from the bags of loot. "But let's not forget why we started this whole trip. I think we should go to a proper holiday location like we'd planned."

"I could go for that," Chuck said. "I can still write my takeover proposal while relaxing."

"Same," Jimmy added. He stood. "I want to go somewhere absolutely crazy."

"You're already crazy," Dave told him. "We've already had a crazy time to get to this point, and you want *more* crazy? You're crazy."

"A wise man once said, 'Who is crazier? The crazy person, or the crazy person who follows him?' I'm only following Eddie and Chuck."

"Well, I'm following Eddie," Chuck said with a shrug.

"But I'm going where I'm told," Eddie protested half-heartedly.

"And none of you can go anywhere without me," Eve said, "so you're all crazy. Now, I've searched my database and found a lovely planet with a great tourist sector. It's called Wamfor, and it has what had been described as the 'biggest, wildest amusement park in the galaxy'."

Dave gulped. "I'll go along, but I'm not crazy enough to get on a roller coaster."

"Whelp," Jimmy said, and quickly dodged a punch in the arm.

"All right," Eddie said loudly to stop the kids fighting. "Wamfor it is."

"Hang on, hang on," Dave said. "Before we go there, I have something I need to do."

"What is it?" Chuck asked.

"I'll tell you on the way. But I think you will all appreciate it."

22

DAVE'S ERRAND

Eddie FLEW OVER A sparkling ocean. It took him a moment to find the place he was looking for. When he did, he settled the ship down in a clearing that was just big enough for his flying watermelon. Dave beckoned his friends to follow him. When they got outside, the humidity smacked them like a hot sponge. There was a commotion up ahead, and Dave led the guys towards it, Cameron buzzing along with them.

In no time at all, the four humans and the camera drone were again face-to-face with the towering figures of the Iwathi people. But instead of attacking them, the aliens dropped down to the ground and performed an act of obeisance. The sea of falling bodies rolled back towards the camp as each new row of Iwathi saw the people they had previously tried to execute and sacrifice, but who had miraculously escaped within the body of their supreme goddess. That physical manifestation of Keovara was right there before them, and they shuddered in reverence.

The Iwathi chief and priestess stepped through to the front of the group of worshippers, eyeing the unannounced visitors. The recognition on their faces was quite visible, as was the veneration they held for *Liberty* in the background. Perhaps humbled by the sudden return of his goddess, the chief prostrated himself, and the priestess followed suit.

This was now Dave's moment. He summoned Cameron to speak for him. "People of the Iwathi tribe," he called. Cameron translated and he saw the alien heads bob up when they were addressed. "Stand," Dave continued, "and see the forgiveness we show to you."

Hesitantly, the aliens stood, then waited intently for what Dave had to say next.

"We hold no grudge against you," Dave said, "for you are all dumb. So we have returned but for a brief moment to pass on this message, and to seal our forgiveness with a lasting gesture of goodwill. Chief Mathai, please step forward."

The chief did so. For the whole journey over to Bolomere, Dave had said nothing of his intentions. In fact, there was some trepidation about coming to the planet where they had nearly been killed. But he'd asked the guys to trust him. They shifted uneasily behind him, wary of the large gathering of once-hostile aliens.

This was all new for Dave. Rarely did he ever take the lead in any of their endeavours, but this time he felt he had a firm grip on what he was doing. If there was anything his trip had taught him, it was that he could do anything with the support of his friends. Their presence alone gave him courage.

With the chief standing close in front of him, Dave turned to face his friends. "This is for the red cheeks they gave us, and for ripping your shirt, Chuck." Then he turned back to the chief and addressed the whole tribe. "On behalf of Keovara, I, Attendant Dave, pass on this official seal of forgiveness to Chief Mathai."

"Dave, are you sure about this?" Eddie asked.

"Never been surer." He looked back at his friends. "We've had a lot of adventures on this trip. But I can tell you now: this is only the beginning."

Dave extended his right arm back as far as it would go, palm out, holding it there for just a second, before whipping forward and up to the chief's waiting face.

Chief Mathai received the most glorious slap any Iwathi had ever seen or experienced.

ACKNOWLEDGEMENTS

I would like to thank my mother for giving birth to me, my father and brother for giving me some good jokes, Abigail Nathan for her editorial work, my sister for her proofreading efforts, Tom Edwards for his fantastic cover art, my beta readers for their helpful and encouraging comments, and everyone who has waited with eager expectation for this book to be published. It has been a long road with a steep learning curve and disruptions in the publishing industry, but I'm glad I could finally release this book to the world.

ABOUT THE AUTHOR

Nick Marone grew up in Sydney, Australia before eventually moving south towards Canberra. He developed an interest in science fiction in his teens and has been hooked ever since. His first book, the novella *Fire Over Troubled Water*, was released in 2019, and he has a growing list of short story sales. Over the years, he has worked for *Aurealis* and *Andromeda Spaceways Magazine*. He hopes to spread laughter and lightheartedness with many more *Space Trip* stories, but also has other serious books in progress.

Learn more about Nick Marone, read interesting and helpful articles on writing, editing, and publishing, and sign up to his free newsletter at **nickmarone.com**. You can also find him on Facebook, Goodreads, and Instagram.

SPACE TRIP II
THE JOURNEY TO FIND THE SECRET OF THE THING IN THE BOX

Following their wild maiden voyage aboard *Liberty* and their impulsive purchase of an abandoned resort city, Dave, Eddie, Jimmy, and Chuck haphazardly embark on a new adventure.

Jimmy buys a mysterious box from a small, unassuming antique shop. When he finally gets it open, the secrets it contains will pull him and his friends into a galaxy-spanning hunt for answers and, hopefully, treasure. All Jimmy wants is a few pots of gold.

But the guys are not the only ones interested in the box and its mesmerising contents. A wealthy collector is on their tail—he cares less about treasure and wants more than just answers.

What's in the box? Why are four hopeless treasure hunters scouring the galaxy to unlock its secrets? Who is their pursuer, why is he after Jimmy's bargain box, and what tricks will he play to get what he wants?

OUT 1 NOVEMBER 2022

SPACE TRIP II

THE JOURNEY TO FIND THE SECRET OF THE THING IN THE BOX

NICK MARONE